'I cannot tell you why you are in danger, but the reason is real. I had hoped that when I came I could let you go, but things did not go according to plan. If you don't want to stay here out of sight, then I have a compromise to offer.'

'What sort of compromise?' she asked suspiciously.

'One you're not going to like, but it is as far as I'm prepared to go. Tomorrow we'll fly back to London and you'll move in with me. I want you to act as my—call it my latest interest—for at least a couple of weeks, possibly longer.'

'What?' Leola had been sure she couldn't feel any more astonishment, but this—this *outrageous* suggestion deprived her of speech again. 'Your latest interest? What the hell does that mean?'

'As my mistress—my lover,' he elaborated...

Robyn Donald has always lived in Northland in New Zealand, initially on her father's stud dairy farm at Warkworth, then in the Bay of Islands, an area of great natural beauty, where she lives today with her husband and an ebullient and mostly Labrador dog. She resigned her teaching position when she found she enjoyed writing romances more, and now spends any time not writing, reading, gardening, travelling, and writing letters to keep up with her two adult children and her friends.

Recent titles by the same author:

HIS MAJESTY'S MISTRESS
VIRGIN BOUGHT AND PAID FOR
THE PRINCE'S CONVENIENT BRIDE

THE
MEDITERRANEAN
PRINCE'S
CAPTIVE VIRGIN

BY
ROBYN DONALD

™ MILLS & BOON®

Pure reading pleasure

First published in Great Britain 2008
Harlequin Mills & Boon Limited,
Eton House, 18-24 Paradise Road, Richmond, Surrey TW9 1SR

© Robyn Donald 2008

ISBN: 978 0 263 20307 3

Set in Times Roman 10½ on 12¾ pt
07-0608-47637

Printed and bound in Great Britain
by Antony Rowe Ltd, Chippenham, Wiltshire

THE
MEDITERRANEAN
PRINCE'S
CAPTIVE VIRGIN

CHAPTER ONE

SHIVERING a little in the night air, Leola Foster stared down into a square dominated on one side by a Romanesque church and on another by a tall stone watchtower. Jagged blocks of stone along the top of the cliff—all that remained of a ruined wall—reminded her that San Giusto, the southernmost city in the Sea Isles of Illyria, had once needed protection from pirates. Spring was only a few weeks old, and even this far south it wasn't really warm enough to stand by the shuttered window in her pyjamas.

But she'd given up trying to get back to sleep. Images from the dream that had jerked her awake still lingered with a sour, humiliating aftertaste. She shivered again, wishing her unconscious would stop replaying the incident over and over again in a never-ending loop.

Call her naïve, she thought with a bitterness that startled her, but she'd never for a moment suspected that Durand had any interest in her; three months ago when she'd arrived in London from New Zealand, her employer's partner—in both personal and business senses—had completely ignored her.

Leola smiled grimly, remembering how excited she'd

been, how confident that this was another step up in her chosen career. After all, Tabitha Grantham was a world-famous brand, noted for the cool sophistication and perfect tailoring of the clothes she designed.

And Tabitha herself had contacted Leola after seeing her line at Auckland's Fashion Week.

'I like your edge,' she'd said, interviewing her over cock-tails in the opulent hotel suite she shared with Durand. 'I think you'll go far and I'd like to help you. You'll learn plenty, but I have to warn you I don't pay my interns much, and I'll expect you to work like a galley slave.'

And work her hard she had. Not that Leola had objected. She'd found it exhilarating, bewildering, shocking and fas-cinating, and she'd soaked up every bit of information she could, every scrap of technique, every contact.

Pity it had all come to an abrupt, mortifying end when Jason Durand decided she'd do as his latest fling.

Unseeing, her gaze skimmed the dark spires of the cy-presses along the ruined wall. Night had worked a transfor-mation on the city. Bustling and noisy and charmingly Mediterranean during the day, San Giusto brooded silently under the Northern hemisphere stars. A violent homesick-ness gripped her; in New Zealand the stars were familiar and the breeze tangy with a wilder, more primal scent.

It was still there, she thought wistfully; she could return any time.

In fact, it looked as though she'd be back there pretty soon. If it hadn't been for the godmother who'd given her this week in Illyria as a birthday present she'd be maxing out her credit card right now on airfares.

Her head came up proudly. No, she would *not* slink back

with her tail between her legs—or not until she'd exhausted every option. She didn't do defeat.

So she'd find new digs first. Without Tabitha's subsidy she couldn't afford the bedsit; she'd had to plead with the landlord to store her suitcases until she came back from this trip.

So digs first, a new job next.

Her lips tightened in a mixture of outrage and frustration. Dammit, she'd been fighting Durand off when Tabitha walked into the room three days ago, yet it had made no difference.

'I'm sorry,' Tabitha had said, her eyes steely, 'but Durand is more important to me than you are. I don't want to see you again.'

Of course Durand was a vital part of the business, but it had been Tabitha's callous dismissal—as though Leola had been a Victorian housemaid found pilfering!—that had stung, enough for her to threaten Durand with the police or the press when he'd refused to pay out her final week's wage.

That had got her the money, but she'd rather have had the internship.

Leola drew in a deep breath of air scented with pine and salt, figs and grape. She was not going to let betrayal or her fear for the future spoil her week in this lovely place, and if she couldn't sleep she might as well work her restlessness off. A brisk walk should do it.

Ten minutes later she locked the door of her apartment behind her and strode towards the deep, mysterious shadows at the base of the ancient tower that marked the cliff walk.

It was a night from an ancient fable—serenely impersonal sky, the soft sigh of the sea on the rocks at the base of the cliff, a stillness so profound she almost expected to see a nymph flit from one of the trees to join her sisters in classical frolics with dolphins.

Yet halfway across the square the skin between Leola's shoulder blades prickled, and she had to resist the urge to swing around and scan the darkened houses behind her.

Cravenly glad that she'd worn a dark top over her black jeans, she was relieved to reach the shade of the trees at the foot of the tower. Slowly, telling herself she was being stupid, she turned.

Her breath stopped in her throat. From the corner of her eye she spotted a stealthy movement at the base of the church. Someone—or something—was sliding along the ancient stone.

So what? It was probably just one of the local dogs coming home from a night on the tiles.

So why was adrenalin pumping through her, quickening her senses, ramping up her pulse so that all she could hear was the rapid, heavy thud of her own heartbeat?

Because her night-attuned eyes picked out people—a line of them, some stumbling, some walking fast, all noiseless. They seemed to emerge from a deeper darkness in the church wall—a door—and they were heading for the wall.

A flare of light shocked her into a gasp; she saw a man's face—handsome, subtly cruel—before the light died.

And then she was grabbed from behind in one swift, brutal movement, an iron hand clamping across her mouth so that her scream had no chance to escape. Instinct drove her to a frenzy of struggling desperation, but she was dragged into the pitch blackness of some recess in the wall.

Think, she commanded herself, and tried to turn so she could knee her captor in the groin, an assault he blocked with ruthless efficiency. She forced herself to go limp, surreptitiously folding her fingers into a fist, but his arms crushed her against a lean, shockingly strong body, completely subduing her so that she could neither move nor signal.

All coherent thought lost to an unnerving panic, she tried biting at the remorseless hand over her mouth, but that didn't work either. It tightened, cutting off her breath.

Panic kicked her ferociously in the stomach and she let herself sag. He eased the pressure a little, but she could feel the tension smoking off him.

A quiet scraping, then what sounded like a muffled curse in an unknown language—Illyrian?—came from the direction of the square. Every muscle painfully taut, Leola waited for some sign of inattention from the man who held her so fiercely against him; he was big, she realised, as well as hugely powerful, and he…

He smelt good.

In some wildly illogical way that clean male scent eased her fear a little.

Until she was hauled sideways, through what had to be a door in the wall. Barely audible, her captor said in English, 'Don't be frightened.'

How did he know she'd understand?

He didn't let her go, and he didn't take his hand away from her mouth. If anything, the fingers tightened a fraction. In warning? Forcing down a spasm of terror, Leola waited for him to lose concentration.

She couldn't see what was happening, but a faint thud sounded as if he'd kicked the door shut behind them and the air became musty. Shivering, she realised they were inside the tower.

'Just another few minutes,' he said again, his words pitched for her ears only. 'Walk.'

Instead Leola sagged, hoping he'd think she'd fainted and that she might get a chance to get away.

It didn't work. Ruthlessly he propelled her in front of him.

'Stairs,' he said, still in that deep, oddly soft voice, half lifting, half dragging her upwards.

Once they reached the top would he throw her down the cliff into the sea below? Panic surged again, freezing her mind.

All she could think of doing was to pretend to find it hard going, stumbling, hesitating, until he said curtly, 'It's no use. And you're safe enough.' His voice was hard and cool and deep, the upper-class English accent very faintly underpinned by something much more exotic.

In spite of her fear she snorted in pure outrage, and he laughed, an oddly amused sound that made her wonder if she was indeed safe. 'OK, we're far enough away now for you not to be heard,' he said, and those cruel fingers relaxed, fell away.

She screamed with every ounce of strength she possessed, only to have it cut off by his hand again.

'Wildcat,' he said, that infuriating note of—mockery?—underlying the single word.

Furiously, she opened her eyes to glare at him. He released her, and, unable to see for a few seconds, she swayed, blinking ferociously until she was finally able to focus on her captor, calmly barring the door behind them. He turned, and her breath locked in her throat.

In the dim light of one electric bulb he looked like something out of a mediaeval epic, a warrior with a warrior's uncompromising ruthlessness. Darkly tanned, with the arrogant facial structure of some Nordic conqueror, he was smiling, but his eyes were hard, an almost translucent ice-grey. And although she was tall herself, Leola had to look a long way up into those piercing eyes.

A feverish shiver—of apprehension, or perhaps recognition—scudded the length of her spine. He was built like a Viking, and the aura of danger pulsing about him made her take a step backwards, although she kept her head high.

'Who are you?' she demanded. 'Why did you drag me up here?'

His gaze sharpening, he bent his black head and said brusquely, 'I hurt you. I'm sorry.'

Leola felt it then, the sting of her cut lip, the taste of blood when she ran her tongue over it. '*You're* sorry? So am I. What the hell do you think you're up to?'

Long tanned fingers dipped into his pocket, producing a handkerchief. 'Here,' he ordered. 'Wipe it.'

Automatically she took the cloth, still warm from his body, and patted her lip. The bloodstain was tiny; showing him, she said, 'It's nothing.'

Her eyes widened as he covered the stone floor between them in two steps to lift her chin in a strong hand, black brows drawing together as he surveyed her face.

'It certainly won't mar your beauty,' he said, and when she flinched he laughed in his throat and bent, kissing the maltreated lip with a gentleness that was very much out of accord with his intimidating appearance.

'What was that for?' she asked inanely, wondering why her legs felt as though the bones had dissolved.

'I kissed it better. Did your mother never do that for you?'

Her mother hadn't been the affectionate sort—not to her

children, anyway. In a brittle voice Leola said, 'It only works if you love the person doing the kissing.'

'I must remember that,' he returned, the sardonic humour vanishing so that she met eyes that were coldly, implacably intent. 'Now, what were you doing walking the square at three-fifteen in the morning?'

'Possibly the same as you,' she countered.

'I hope not.' He paused to lethal effect before prompting silkily, 'Tell me.'

Leola masked an involuntary stab of fear with a shrug. 'It's no big deal. I couldn't sleep. None of the books I brought were worth reading again and I didn't fancy a hot drink, so I decided to go for a walk. What's so unusual about that?'

'Did you hear or see anything?'

'Yes,' she said smartly. 'I was attacked by a total stranger and dragged into a tower.'

His humourless smile showed very white teeth. 'This is important,' he said, each word a warning.

'Why?' Her heart picked up speed as another surge of adrenalin activated her flight-or-fight response.

Fighting was useless; he'd already shown her a measure of his strength, nicely judged so as not to hurt her too badly. A swift shiver scudded down her spine at the memory of that oddly tender kiss.

Flight, then? Hastily she glanced around. The room he'd brought her to was made of stone, its only obvious exit the door they'd come through. He'd haul her away from that before she could lift the bar. Shadows hid the farthest wall, but her quick glance and the musty air told her there were no windows.

Flight seemed impossible too.

The cold pool beneath her ribs expanded. What had she unwittingly walked into? Strangely, instinct told her that this man wasn't a direct threat to her safety, but one glance at his flint-hard face with its arrogant bone structure reminded her that sometimes instinct couldn't be trusted.

'Did you see any movement?' he asked, quite gently, but something in his icy regard warned her not to lie.

Eyes troubled, she hesitated. 'How do I know if you're one of the good guys?'

Damn, Nico thought, he liked her spirit, even if it was extremely inconvenient. Just before he'd kissed her—an impulse he should have resisted—he'd noticed that her eyes were a dark blue-green with intriguing gold speckles. They were shadowed now, and her full mouth, scratched by his grip, was set in a straight line, her lithe figure stiff and wary.

He repressed his intensely physical reaction. Nico had learned in a hard school not to trust anyone—not even a blonde goddess with an intriguing accent, tawny-gold hair and a body that promised sensual rapture.

'You don't,' he told her without hesitation. 'Tell me what you saw.'

For several moments more her eyes challenged him, and then she made a rapid gesture, instantly cut short. 'Movement,' she said steadily. 'A slow sort of glide along the base of the church.'

Had she decided to trust him? It didn't matter. 'Any faces?'

When she hesitated again he knew she'd seen the man he was tracking. Some poor devil, he thought grimly, would pay for releasing the ray of light that had caught Paveli's fleshy face.

But she said nothing. He scrutinised her guarded face, and

made up his mind. If she was one of Paveli's lookouts she had to be neutralised. If she wasn't, she was in danger. Either way, she had to be removed. 'I'm afraid I'll have to interrupt your holiday for a few days.'

Unable to hide a flash of alarm, she stiffened. 'It's all right,' he assured her, his tone casual. 'You'll be living in a very comfortable house with pleasant people; you just won't be able to leave it.'

'In other words I'll be a prisoner,' she said evenly.

He had to admire her refusal to be daunted and her ability to face facts. 'I'd rather you thought of yourself as a guest,' he said with smooth cynicism, and waited for her response.

'Guests can leave whenever they want to,' she retorted. 'What is this all about?'

'If I told you I'd have to kill you.'

How many times had she heard that tossed at someone in jest? Leola looked at the dark, formidable face of the man who'd hauled her here, and felt the hair on the back of her neck lift. She suspected he meant it.

'You will be perfectly safe,' he said.

'Somehow,' she returned cuttingly, 'I don't find that very reassuring.'

'If it's any consolation, I won't be there.'

She shrugged, although a swift pang of apprehension tightened her nerves. 'It would certainly be more to my liking, but I'm not going anywhere with you.'

'If I have to I'll tie you hand and foot, gag you and blindfold you.' Not a threat, not a warning, just a simple statement of fact not softened by his final words. 'I don't want to do that.'

Apprehension intensifying into something more than

fear, Leola met implacable eyes, cold as polar seas. 'What's the alternative?'

'You give me your word not to scream or make a fuss.'

'You'd accept my word?'

His smile was humourless. 'I'll still have to gag and blindfold you, but we could dispense with the hog-tying.'

Anger helped drown out the terror. From between her teeth she ground out, 'I refuse to help you kidnap me. What sort of fool do you think I am?'

'One that's entirely too mouthy,' he said, and kissed her—not the gentle kiss of the previous time but a full-on plundering of her mouth as though he had every right to do it, as though they were passionate lovers separated for years and at last together again.

Fire leapt through her, replacing cold panic with an emotion just as primal, just as overriding—a heady, violent desire that sang like some siren's potent, dangerous song.

With every bit of will she possessed Leola resisted the astonishing, rising tide of passion, until she felt a sharp prick in her neck.

Stomach contracting in wild terror, she forced open her eyes to stare at him.

'You're going to be all right,' he said, his voice suddenly harsh. 'Don't be afraid.'

The meaningless words echoed in her mind as darkness rolled over her.

Nico held her until she went limp, then looked at the man who'd come in through the secret passage. The newcomer was lowering a hypodermic.

In the local dialect Nico said, 'Does it always work so fast?'

'She must be very susceptible.'

'Thank you, my friend,' Nico said grimly. 'How the hell did you happen to have this drug on your person?'

'I always carry it. I am, after all, a doctor. It's just as quick as hitting someone over the head, and less noisy.' His companion gave a laconic grin. 'That one would have fought all the way. You must be losing your touch.'

'She was afraid,' Nico said absently, looking down at her white face. Even deeply unconscious, she was beautiful. Something hot and unguarded stirred inside him; it had been too long since he'd had a lover.

Controlling it, he went on, 'Thank you for that—we can't afford to either waste time on her or have her caught.'

'Do you think she is in league with Paveli?' The doctor said the name like a curse. 'She could have been acting as a lookout.'

Nico frowned. 'I don't know.'

'Perhaps she's his woman. We know nothing about her.'

'Her accent says she's a New Zealander. It seems unlikely she has anything to do with him, but she saw Paveli in the square, and she wasn't going to tell me.'

The newcomer stared at the woman, and, moved by some feeling he didn't explore, Nico adjusted her limp body so that her face was hidden against his chest. 'We have to get her out of here,' he said brusquely, and lifted her.

Fragrant against him, she lay in his arms as though she belonged there. Grimly Nico controlled his swift, fierce response and headed for the opening to the secret passage.

'And you, my Lord, are altogether too recognisable,' the doctor said briskly from behind.

Nico's arms tightened around the woman in his arms. 'So we'll make sure she's safe until we can ask her a few more questions.'

* * *

Leola woke to a throbbing head and a dry mouth; when she tried to lift her eyelids that hurt her head even more. Without volition she groaned.

From somewhere close by a woman said in heavily accented English, 'You feel bad now, but soon you will be better. Drink this.'

Leola sipped greedily, then sank back into sleep, tossing restlessly as a hard-eyed Viking prowled through her dreams.

When she woke again she lay very still, forcing her sluggish brain into action. Slowly, reluctantly, it disgorged memories—her decision to go for a walk at night, and a face revealed by a flare of light. She shivered, because something about that face filled her with repugnance.

The image was replaced by another face—hard, forcefully handsome, compelling.

Ice-grey eyes, she thought, the pictures jumbling in her brain. He'd kissed her and all hell had broken loose...

Had he hit her over the head? A tentative hand revealed no sore spot there.

Drugs, then...

Dimly she remembered a sharp pain in her neck while he was kissing her. Her captor hadn't been waving a hypodermic around, so someone else must have come up from behind.

Her captor's kiss had been a cynical ploy to dazzle her into mindless submission.

Humiliatingly, it had worked. Shame ate into her; she'd known he was dangerous, yet she'd succumbed to his cynical caress like some raw teenager awash with hormones.

Never again, she vowed.

At least it didn't seem as though he intended to kill her.

On the other hand she might be a hostage or a bargaining tool. Or he might just fancy a playmate for a few nights before getting rid of her.

Feeling sick, she shifted uneasily, wondering if he'd already...

No, she felt entirely normal, just lax and sleepy. Surely she'd know if she'd been raped?

How? Although she'd had plenty of men friends, several of whom would have liked to become closer, she'd been too dedicated—too intensely focused on her dreams and her career—for relationships.

Too scared, too; long ago she'd decided that love and passion led to pain and humiliation. So, as one-night stands were definitely not her style, she was that *rare thing in the modern world*, a virgin.

But it hadn't been fear she'd felt when the grey-eyed Viking had kissed her, and his kisses had wiped any thought of career and ambition from her mind. His kisses had made her feel uncontrolled and wanton and desirous.

No other man had ever done that.

Whatever she'd walked into last night in the square, she didn't want a bar of it. She had to get away from here— wherever *here* was!

Feverish thoughts jostled through her brain, but in the end the only plan she could come up with was to pretend to be the idiot her captor no doubt thought her.

Feigning sleep, she tried to gather as many sensory impressions as she could. She was in a bed—a very comfortable one. Outside she could hear what seemed to be the soft lapping of water, but there was no smell of salt. Instead, an indescribable freshness filled the air, mingled with the now familiar scents of cypresses and something lighter and sweeter. Flowers?

And someone else was with her. Although the room was silent, she could just catch the faint rhythm of something making regular motions. A rocking chair, she thought, rather pleased with herself for working this out.

She simply couldn't imagine the man who'd brought her here in a rocking-chair. Oddly enough that thought brought a smile to the corners of her mouth, and gave her the courage to slowly, stealthily, lift her lashes. This time they obeyed her will, so that she could see the woman who sat sewing beside a long window.

Nothing frightening there, she thought with a swift rush of relief. Middle-aged, pleasantly plump, clad in some sort of nurse's uniform, the woman in the chair wore her black hair off her face in a bun at her neck. Her olive skin and Mediterranean features meant she was probably Illyrian.

As though she was warned by some sixth sense, the woman's head swung abruptly around, her face lighting up when she saw Leola watching her.

'Ah, you are truly awake,' she said, and came across to stand beside her, automatically taking her wrist and checking her pulse.

'Where am I?' Leola's voice sounded croaky and feeble at the same time.

'In Osita, in the Sea Isles,' the woman told her readily, re-leasing her wrist. 'Yes, you are feeling much better. Perhaps you would like something to eat, hmm?'

Osita? Leola frowned, trying to remember where she'd seen that name, then discarded the search to concentrate on more important things. Although the thought of food nauseated her, if she said yes, the nurse might leave the room to collect it.

And then she could get up to work out where she was. 'I'll try,' she said cautiously.

But the woman rang a bell beside the bed. 'Something light would be best. Soup, I think.'

Baulked, Leola said in a muted voice, 'Thank you.'

Almost immediately there came a knock at a door. The nurse bustled across and ordered whatever it was she'd decided on, then came back. 'So, let me help you sit up,' she said. 'You will want to wash your face and clean your teeth. I will bring you a basin.'

After helping Leola sit against a bank of pillows, she went off through another door, this one in the wall opposite.

Turning her head carefully, Leola examined the large, beautifully furnished room. No prison cell this, she thought with a stab of unwanted appreciation. It was a sumptuously decorated bedroom—a woman's room. The large glass doors opened out onto a balcony; through the balustrade she could see the tops of trees, and a glimpse of blue, blue water against forested hills.

Not the sea, though; a lake. And a picture suddenly flicked up in her mind—a lake amongst hills, with a small island to one side. And on the island a castle set in gardens.

A very good place to keep a prisoner, she thought grimly, wondering how far from the shores of the lake the island was. She'd seen the photograph of Osita in a tourist brochure, but since she'd had no intention of going there she'd taken little interest in it.

The nurse brought her the basin and a hairbrush, and

stood by while she freshened up before brushing her hair into some sort of order.

'So pretty,' the woman commented as Leola smoothed the tawny-gold locks back from her face.

Absurdly self-conscious, Leola said, 'Thank you.' And asked before she could think things through, 'Who owns this place?'

The woman looked surprised. 'The prince,' she said, as though there was only one prince and everyone knew his name.

While Leola digested this in dumbfounded silence, another knock on the door summoned her keeper across to collect a tray.

The *prince*? The only prince she could think of was Prince Roman, the hereditary ruler of the Illyrian Sea Isles, and she'd seen photographs of him. With the stunning good looks of some Mediterranean god, he wasn't her Viking.

Fugitive colour burned across her cheeks as she realised what her wayward mind had come up with. Whoever the man who'd brought her here was, he most definitely wasn't *her* anything.

After all, he'd kissed her just so that someone could pump her full of drugs. But if this place belonged to Prince Roman Magnati surely she couldn't be in any real danger. He'd grown up in Switzerland, become a tycoon, and only recently returned to Illyria to take over his duties and responsibilities.

It didn't seem likely he'd be any sort of threat. But in that case, why was she here?

CHAPTER TWO

LEOLA looked up as the nurse returned and settled the tray over her knees. Her worried thoughts took second place to hunger. Lemons, she thought, and chicken—and some sort of very tiny pasta? Certainly a hint of garlic.

'Eggs and lemon soup with chicken,' the nurse told her. 'A Greek dish, and good for illness—very soothing and nourishing.'

Amazingly, Leola finished it, and the chunk of crusty bread that arrived with it, obediently ate an orange and drank a cup of coffee with milk and sugar. Even more amazingly she drifted off into a restful sleep afterwards.

It wasn't until the second day that she wondered if she was being drugged with a mild sedative. Those naps were too frequent. She tried to convince herself that it could be the after-effects of the original drug, and waited for the nurse to leave the room. Cautiously, head spinning rather pleasantly, she got out of bed—and found herself staggering like a drunkard.

Something was definitely wrong.

Apart from the obvious physical effects, she felt altogether too mellow. Normally she'd be spitting tacks at this impri-sonment; now she could barely summon up any resentment.

And it was *not* because the Viking kept striding into her thoughts and her dreams…

Clutching the back of an armchair, she stared out the window and took in a series of deep breaths, forcing herself to concentrate. The scene outside was magnificent, gardens and lawns bordered by huge trees that almost hid what seemed to be a small building, perhaps a chapel, built in the same pale stone as the castle.

But tempting though it was to drink it all in, she couldn't waste time on the beauty spread before her.

Although she couldn't see any sign of a jetty, presumably there was one hidden by the trees. She leaned forward, frowning as she estimated the distance between the island and the mainland.

Too far for her to cross without transport. Having been brought up beside the sea, she was a good swimmer, but she wouldn't manage that distance.

Even her disappointment was muted. Angrily, she called on her strength to resist the effects of whatever drug she'd ingested. Perhaps the other side of the island was closer to the shore. If it was less than a kilometre she'd be all right.

So she'd find out. She'd insist on taking a walk. But she'd need to get the drug out of her system first; right now she was too limp to cope with anything more than a leisurely stroll, let alone a lengthy swim.

It was no use asking the nurse for help, since she had to be administering the sedative.

Just you wait, Prince Whoever-you-are, she thought fiercely. One day you'll regret you ever dragged me into this business.

The door opened behind her. She turned, almost over-balancing as her head whirled. Grimly she clung to the back of the armchair, taking another deep breath until her vision settled down.

After a soft exclamation the nurse crossed the big room remarkably fast. 'I think you try too hard, too soon,' she chided, her dark eyes concerned. 'Come, I'll help you into the chair.'

Shaken, Leola let her, and once settled into the armchair decided that from now on she'd eat as little as possible and drink only water she'd run herself from the tap.

The nurse brought her several English magazines—fashion magazines Leola had already seen. She flicked through them, measuring the impact of various outfits, enjoying one acerbic column again, frowning at others, before pushing the magazines aside.

Focus on figuring out a way to get yourself out of here, she commanded herself.

Because she was going to have to. If she didn't return home on her due date from this holiday no questions would be asked, no people alerted by her absence. She bit her lip. Well, not until her twin sister in New Zealand realised something was wrong.

Which could already have happened, she thought anxiously. They shared a link; what one felt the other recognised. Oh, Lord, she hoped Giselle wasn't frantically trying to contact her. Then her mouth curled ironically. On the other hand, that would mean release was close, because no prince would be a match for Giselle on the warpath.

Tense with anger and frustration at her growing feeling of impotence, she picked up another magazine, flipping angrily through the pages until her eyelids grew heavy and her head slid sideways.

She woke with a clearer brain and sight; a quick glance around the room revealed that she was alone again. This time she wasn't nearly as shaky as she stood up from the chair and made her way into the bathroom to get a glass of water.

Once it had been thirstily drained, she looked down at herself. She still wore the same exquisitely embroidered nightdress she'd woken in, and today, she decided, she was going to demand some clothes.

And a walk in the garden.

Plus, she was going to demand to know exactly why Prince Whoever had had her brought here, and what the hell was going on!

She was back in the bedroom when the nurse tapped on the door and entered, beaming at the sight of her charge on her feet. 'You feel better now?' she asked. 'Good. I run water for you in the bath, and then you can get dressed.'

Without waiting for an answer, the woman bustled into the bathroom, humming as she went.

Leola gave a wry grin. So much for her new-found assertiveness! Clearly not needed at all. But a bath would be wonderful in that superb Victorian bath on its four lion feet...

'It's ready,' the nurse said, reappearing. 'You want me to bathe you?'

Leola said hastily, 'No, thanks, I'll be fine.' She sniffed appreciatively. 'What did you put in the water? It smells divine.'

'Oh, something the girls here use to make themselves smell good,' the nurse said with another smile. 'From flowers that grow in the hills.' She nodded and left the room.

Although Leola was still shaky when she finally got out, she did feel much stronger, and her brain seemed to be working with something like its usual speed.

After drying herself with the sumptuous towels she donned the silk dressing gown that had been left for her and walked out into the bedroom, where the nurse indicated a pair of trousers, a silk shirt and underclothes laid out on the newly made bed.

All, she noted, brand-new. And her heart skipped a beat when she recognised the designer—Magda Wright, one of Europe's most respected, who had made her name and her fortune by dressing Europe's aristocracy and royalty. Her signature butterfly adorned the pocket of the silk shirt and the waistband of the trousers.

'They're not mine,' Leola said, uncertain how to deal with this.

The older woman nodded. 'For you,' she said firmly.

Leola hesitated, but she needed clothes in her campaign to make herself familiar with her prison. Nevertheless…

'Where are my own clothes?'

The nurse looked wary. 'I do not know,' she finally said.

Leola frowned down at the garments. 'Who brought these?' she asked.

'The prince sent them,' the nurse said, as though Leola should have known who the donor was.

'What prince?'

This time the woman looked nervous. 'The Prince of the Sea Isles,' she said eventually.

'Prince Roman Magnati?' Leola held her breath.

'Oh, no. Prince Nico Magnati. His younger brother.' The nurse's sweeping gesture took in the room, the palace and the glorious view outside. 'Prince Roman is prince over all the Sea Isles, but this—all this place belongs to Prince Nico.'

The Viking?

A dim recollection of reading about a playboy prince fired some brain cells. 'I see,' Leola said, looking down at the bra. She didn't need to read the label to know that it was her size. A kind of dark anger smouldered into life inside her.

Such accuracy meant that whoever had estimated her size was altogether too familiar with women's bodies.

But of course playboys would be. She searched her mind, trying to locate the source of that tenuous conviction, only to give up when the nurse went to tidy the bathroom.

Her head still buzzing with questions, Leola checked the clothes, somehow not surprised that both the beautifully cut trousers and shirt were her exact size.

So was her Viking Prince Nico Magnati, younger brother of the Lord of the Sea Isles?

She recalled the effortlessly commanding air of the man who'd snatched her from the square and sent her here. Yes, that fitted someone of aristocratic heritage, but although princes certainly had power, she doubted whether many of them possessed that fierce aura of danger, of disturbing sexuality.

And why on earth would a prince be involved in cloak-and-dagger stuff? They had minions for that sort of thing, surely?

Biting her lip, she walked across to the window. At first she didn't register what she was seeing until the movement caught her attention, and she realised a fast motorboat was clipping through the water towards the island.

Her stomach hollowed out in something close to panic. She turned to the nurse, who hurried across and stood just behind her.

'The prince,' she announced happily.

And realising Leola was still standing in a dressing gown,

she gestured at the clothes she'd laid out. 'Quickly, quickly, before he comes.'

Heart beating with heavy impact, Leola scrambled into the clothes, some inner part of her relishing the sleek luxury of silk against her skin, even though she hated the thought of being dressed by a man who'd treated her with such cavalier authority.

The nurse disappeared while Leola grimly combed her hair and smoothed it back from her face. When she found herself tugging the same tawny-gold lock of hair for the third time, she bit her lip. Both the tugging and the biting were left-overs from her childhood methods of diffusing stress, and neither worked. She eased back into the armchair, took several deep, slow breaths, then deliberately relaxed every muscle in her body.

That didn't work either.

Tension built exponentially until the nurse appeared again, and said without her usual smile, 'The prince will see you now.'

But when Leola got out of the chair, the older woman shook her head. 'He will come here.'

It was clear from her tone that she didn't approve, and equally clear that she didn't feel she could do anything about it.

'Very well,' Leola said, her voice too thin. She swallowed again and walked across to the window, standing with her back to the glorious view outside so that she could watch the door without her own expression being too clear.

Apprehension pooled beneath her ribs. She wondered whether she'd be disappointed or relieved—or just plain spitting furious—if the man who came in through the door was the Viking.

He appeared so swiftly, so silently, that her pulse jumped; one moment she was alone, the next he was in the room with her, radiating that unmistakable, intimidating aura of formidable power.

'So you're Prince Nico Magnati,' she said unsteadily.

The Viking smiled. 'For my sins, yes.' His cool grey eyes scanned her face. 'How is your lip?'

Colour burned through her skin when she remembered the tiny scratch, and his kiss.

'It's fine, but *I'm* pretty shaky,' she flashed, adding caustically, 'thanks to whatever sedative you've had me pumped full of.'

'I wondered when you'd work it out.' His ironic smile irritated her at the same time as it set off small clusters of fireworks in her veins. 'Maria tells me you haven't eaten much today.'

'I don't like being force-fed drugs. Why?'

Broad shoulders sketched a wholly Mediterranean shrug, yet there was nothing casual in his gaze or his tone. 'If you hadn't been quite so articulate and stroppy when we first met I might not have felt it necessary, but I guessed you were not someone I could persuade easily to keep out of sight for several days.'

'You were right,' she said coldly. 'Why was it necessary?'

'Because if it had become known that you'd been out and about at that time on that night you'd have been—in fact, you probably are still—in some danger.'

Although he spoke levelly, without inflection, something in his tone, in the way he looked at her, made her go cold. He meant it.

Still in that same dispassionate tone he resumed, 'I think

I got you out of sight before anyone noticed you, but I'm not sure. It was better for you to disappear.'

'And how did you explain my absence to my landlord and his family?' she asked with chilly politeness.

The prince gave a sudden, sexy grin. 'That was easy. I merely sent a maid to collect your clothes and let her tell them that you and I planned to spend the rest of your holiday together. It seemed the most likely explanation for your disappearance,' he finished blandly, obviously amused by her reaction.

Outrage rendered her wordless. All she could think of to say was *How dare you!* and she wasn't going to fall back on clichés.

And if she let her temper get the better of her, she'd be putting herself at a huge disadvantage. Prince Nico didn't look as though he let anything crack that steely control.

In the end she demanded, 'Why didn't you send my clothes here too?'

'I didn't want anyone finding out where you were, so in case I was being watched I had them forwarded to my yacht, which is cruising towards Morocco with us supposedly enjoying a passionate affair on it.'

Eyes glittering, she said with searing sarcasm, 'Presumably people believe this story because you make a habit of kidnapping women?'

'Not a habit,' he drawled, eyes hardening. 'So far you're the only one it's been necessary to actually kidnap. My amours have always been with willing women.'

Colour scorched her skin. She said between her teeth, 'So tell me why it was necessary to go to such enormous trouble.'

'No.' He let that sink in, then added, 'Instead, you are going to tell me exactly what you saw in the square the other night.'

It was a direct order. The hairs on the back of her neck lifted, partly in anger, partly because something in his expression warned her that he wasn't going to be put off.

Leola narrowed her eyes, scanning the angular sculpture of his features with an intensity that surprised her. Could she trust him? 'This is important?'

'It is very important.'

'Why should I trust you after all you've done to me?'

'I can give you no reason. But know this, Leola Foster, I am being as honest as I dare to be with you, and whatever I have done, I have done in your best interests.'

They locked gazes like bitter antagonists, hers challenging and wary, his cold and completely determined.

In the end, she said quietly, 'I told you what I saw.'

'Everything?'

She thought of the face she'd seen, sharply defined in the sudden flare of light. The face of an exploiter, she thought, sensual and cruel.

She dragged in a jagged breath. 'You must have seen it too.'

'Tell me.'

Reluctantly she said, 'Just before you grabbed me, I noticed a sort of blur of movement beneath that big cypress tree at the base of the church tower.'

'What sort of movement?'

Frowning, she tried to remember. 'It was people, but they seemed to have manifested themselves out of the air. And they didn't make any noise. I couldn't hear anything except waves on the rocks at the bottom of the cliff.'

'Where were they going?'

'Towards the cliff.'

As far as she knew there was no path down to the coast

there; why would anyone want to clamber down to rocks when on the other side of the narrow peninsula there was a smooth white sand beach from a travel agent's dream?

Slowly she said, 'But if they were actually going to be picked up by a boat they'd have used the port. Unless they didn't want to be seen.'

'And that's all you saw—a blur of movement?'

How much should she tell him? Tensely, torn between a lingering fear and her strange inclination to trust him, she glanced again at his face. The powerfully honed bone structure gave him an intimidating aura of tough ruthlessness that she knew to be well earned. He'd kidnapped and drugged her, but in spite of that and his arrogant and uncompromising aura he looked... *clean*.

It was an odd word, yet it was the only one she could come up with. And she had only her sensory impressions to go on.

If they'd met in other circumstances she'd trust him, she thought, wondering if she was being stupid. Nevertheless, she made up her mind. 'Someone must have switched on a torch for a moment. I saw a man's face; it looked vaguely familiar, as though I might have seen him on television, or in the newspapers.'

'And you still have no idea who he might have been?'

She stared accusingly at her inquisitor. 'No. You saw him too, because you grabbed me the moment the torch was turned off.'

Ignoring her comment, he stated briefly, 'I'm afraid you'll have to stay here until it's safe for me to let you go.'

All emotion was stripped from his voice, from his eyes, leaving nothing but a cold authority that blazed forth like a beacon.

Chilled but determined, Leola said firmly, 'I can't stay here. I have to go back to London.'

His brows met across the arrogant blade of his nose. 'Why?'

Because she needed to find a job before the last money in her account was used up. 'That's obvious—I'm due to leave Illyria in a couple of days, and if I miss my flight I can't afford a new ticket, or to stay here.' She drew a breath and lied, 'Besides, I have a career.'

'I don't charge for my hospitality,' he said coolly, adding, 'and you have lost your position in London.'

'How do you—?' Furious with herself, she stopped, staring at him with narrowed, glittering eyes. Her voice tightened. 'You've had me investigated? How dare you? That's utterly—'

'I know you were sacked,' he cut in. 'There is no reason for you to go back just yet.'

'I'm not staying here.'

His face hardened. 'You will do what I choose,' he said implacably.

'You can't do this.'

His mouth tucked in at the corners. 'Who is going to stop me?'

Fury overrode the remnants of discretion, but before she could tell him exactly what she thought of him he held up one large, frighteningly strong hand.

'Listen to me, and think with your head, not your emotions,' he said curtly. 'I cannot tell you why you are in danger but the danger is real, and it is bigger and more important than your natural anger at being held here against your will. I had hoped that when I came I could let you go, but things did not go according to plan. If you don't want to stay here out of sight, then I have a compromise to offer.'

'What sort of compromise?' she asked suspiciously.

'One you're not going to like, but it is as far as I'm prepared to go. Tomorrow we'll fly back to London and you'll move in with me. I want you to act as my—call it my latest interest—for at least a couple of weeks, possibly longer.'

'What?' Leola had been sure she couldn't feel any more astonishment, but this—this *outrageous* suggestion deprived her of speech again. 'Your latest interest? What the hell does that mean?'

'As my mistress—lover, new best friend—whatever,' he elaborated, his tone cool and inflexible.

'No.'

'Then—you stay here.' He smiled without humour when her head came up and her chin jutted, and his eyes were cold when he added, 'Osita is lovely in the spring. Cyclamen and crocuses bloom everywhere—'

'I can't stay here,' she stated, frustrated and furious together, and afraid, because in spite of his dangerous charm there was something completely, coldly implacable in his tone. 'If I don't go back people will notice. The police will be contacted.'

She hoped.

He said coolly, 'I can assure you, once I let it be known that you've decided to extend your holiday for a time as my guest, everyone will accept that.' Cynically he finished, 'Even if you were still working for Tabitha Grantham she would accept your absence in the hope that you'd bring added sales.'

Leola's hands clenched at her sides. Reluctantly she

admitted that he was correct; Tabitha would have consi-
dered her temporary absence as the lover of a very rich man
to be an excellent career move.

The Magnati princes were not just rich—they had huge
power and influence, and they were part of a very exclusive
upper circle, being related to most of the royal houses in
Europe.

If she moved—even for a few weeks—in their world,
she'd have gone from being a nobody from the other side of
the world to a person with valuable contacts...

Not that it mattered any more, since Tabitha had dumped
her. 'My landlord—'

'Was told by your employer that your tenancy had been
terminated the day you came to the Sea Isles.'

Leola felt herself being backed inexorably into a corner.
Flushed and angry, she blurted the first thing that came to
mind. 'It wouldn't work. I'm no actress and we don't know
each other—'

Then she stopped, eyes widening as he advanced across
the room in long, silent strides, his expression decisive.
Nervously she licked her lips, and saw his ironic glance take
in the betraying little movement.

He stopped in front of her, just close enough to remind
her that even when he'd abducted her so brutally she'd
noticed his subtle masculine scent. Her heart quickened,
and her gaze slid down so that he couldn't read what she
was thinking.

'You'll be perfectly safe with me,' he said quietly. 'I told you
I prefer willing women. For your own safety, this is necessary.'

Her voice uncertain, Leola asked, 'Why won't you tell me
what's going on?'

He scanned her face with penetrating eyes, as though he could see into her soul. 'Because you're safer not knowing. You do have a choice, Leola Foster. You can either agree to stay with me in London, or stay here as my guest.'

Take it or leave it, his tone implied, leaving no room for negotiation.

Pride fought with pragmatism. If she agreed to his suggestion she'd be for ever tarred with the stigma of being his temporary mistress. If she refused, she'd be stuck here until he let her go—and who knew how long that might be?

In London at least she'd be able to look for another job and try to find accommodation.

As though he could read her mind he said casually, 'When this is over, I might be of some use in helping you find another position, possibly even better than the one you were so unceremoniously relieved of.'

She bit her lip, ambition warring with a cold common sense that told her nobody got something for nothing. 'You don't have to do that. I can make it on my own.'

Of course it would be much, much easier if she had Prince Nico Magnati batting for her. It galled her that she'd end up with the stigma of being a discarded mistress without the pleasure—

Whoa! No, it didn't. The last thing she needed was any sort of romance with him.

Abruptly she made up her mind.

'Is there anything illegal in what you're doing?' she asked abruptly, watching him keenly.

'No.' The denial was prompt and uncompromising.

Instinct told Leola she could trust him; she hoped it

wasn't influenced by her humiliating physical response to him. 'Morally ambiguous?' she pressed.

He shrugged. 'Possibly, because I am forcing you to choose between two equally distasteful alternatives. However, as each will protect you from possible death, I feel that the risk is worth it.'

'Death?' She felt the colour fade from her skin, but rallied to say disbelievingly, 'Oh, come on…'

CHAPTER THREE

HER words died away when Prince Nico took her chin. 'Look at me,' he commanded.

Leola swallowed but lifted her lashes. His eyes had darkened into an intensity that defeated the defiance sparking through her.

'I am not fooling,' he said quietly. 'Death—your death—is a possibility.'

Desperately, she argued, 'But all I saw was a face.'

'That is more than enough to put your life in danger if the wrong people suspect it.'

Leola's anger transmuted into apprehension. 'So am I ever going to be safe?'

'Yes. Soon he will be in custody. Until then I will protect you. Also, I will be honest; this might not be necessary. Possibly no one was aware of your presence in the square, but the people involved are ruthless; they have killed before, and would kill again if they knew what you saw. Lives are at stake—lives and money and futures.'

'Do you know who that man is?'

He released her, standing back a step. In a voice that gave her no leeway, he said, 'Why do you ask?'

'You do know him, don't you? So are you in danger too?'

One black brow arched in sardonic amusement. 'I can protect myself.' His expression hardened. 'Come, make up your mind. Either you stay here, or in London with me—which is it to be?'

Leola hesitated. 'I'll need to look for another job,' she said, despising herself for surrendering.

'The same sort of thing you had before?'

'If it's at all possible.' Why was he interested? 'Work experience,' she stressed.

Preferably with someone who wasn't interested in women, she thought bitterly.

'Very well, then, but not until this is over and you are safe.'

He meant it. When she opened her mouth he cut in, 'That is non-negotiable. You are in danger, Leola. Accept it.'

Her gaze flew upwards; in his eyes she saw a bleak conviction that iced through her. After a few moments' further struggle with herself, she reluctantly said, 'I don't appear to have much choice. I'll go with you.'

An hour later she decided waspishly that life amongst the rich and powerful had certain advantages. She was sitting in a sleek corporate jet, watching Europe slide beneath her. Not far away the prince was speed-reading his way through what seemed to be a huge pile of documents.

Tea had been offered, and accepted with gratitude in the hope that it might help to clear a mind still clouded by whatever drug Nico Magnati had administered to her.

As if he could read her mind he looked up, the half-smile curving his sculpted mouth fading when he met her accusing glare. 'Are you all right?'

'Yes, although it's no thanks to you,' she said stiffly.

That black brow climbed, but he knew what she was referring to. 'I'm sorry it had to be done, but I didn't trust anyone on the island to keep you there if you made up your mind to leave. You will soon be free of any after-effects.'

'I hope so,' she told him, stopping because the steward appeared with a tray of food.

'Eat now,' Prince Nico commanded.

It wasn't difficult; the snacks were delicious, about as far removed from the usual airline fodder as diamonds from glass. Her tension faded, only to surge back when they approached London, increasing in quantum leaps when she found herself in a magnificent house in Mayfair.

The prince showed her to a bedroom that impressed her with its superb fittings, although she preferred the one in Osita because of its view.

'I suggest you have a shower and a rest,' he said, adding with a smile she found unnecessarily sarcastic, 'and I hope you won't refuse just because I suggested it. Flying dehydrates.'

'I'm not in the habit of cutting off my nose to spite my face,' she returned, a splash of acid in her words.

'Then we should deal very well together.' He indicated a door in the wall. 'Your bathroom and wardrobe are in there. You will be pleased to know that I had someone bring your clothes from your previous lodging and hang them for you.'

'How—?'

His smile turned cynical. 'The landlord was most obliging,' he said and went out, closing the door behind him.

Leola did feel better once she'd worked out how to get the shower going, but she started yawning again when she got into a camisole top and briefs. It was a relief to see familiar clothes hanging in the huge walk-in wardrobe.

They'd been pressed, she noted, wondering who'd done it, and smiled wryly. Certainly not the prince.

Back in the palatial bedroom she noticed that someone had turned back the covers and put a tray on a table beside an armchair with a carafe of water and some fruit and crackers.

Still wary, she ignored them, getting herself a glass of water from the bathroom, and then, with a sigh of relief, crawled between the sheets and fell asleep almost instantly.

The sound of her own name woke her. 'Leola,' someone was saying. 'Wake up, or you won't sleep at all tonight.'

And when she groaned and turned over and buried her face in the pillow, Prince Nico repeated on a note of amusement, 'Leola. Leola, look at me.'

'Go 'way,' she muttered.

But her body responded to his presence before her sluggish brain. A sizzle of electricity powered through her, alerting her to the fact that Nico Magnati was sitting on the side of the bed.

Gently he shook the bare shoulder presented to him. 'Wake up. Or do you want to have dinner in bed?'

'No.'

She barely knew what she'd said; his touch set off fires deep in the pit of her stomach that galvanised her into action. Shocked, she rolled away from him, only to realise that the sheet had slipped and she had on nothing but the skimpy camisole and matching briefs.

Her eyes flew open. Prince Nico was looking at her face, not, she was grateful to see, at her almost exposed breasts, but the glittering heat in his eyes both scared and elated her. Some deeply hidden part of her had recognised the sexuality in his touch, and thrilled to it.

You want him, she thought, appalled and terrified by the swift firestorm of sensation leaping from cell to cell, nerve to nerve. Scarlet-faced, she grabbed the sheet and hauled it up to her chin.

Nico said something in a language she didn't know and she gabbled, 'Get out of here! What do you think you're doing? You told me you'd be—I'd be…'

The tumbling words faltered to a stop. Eyes locked, for long seconds neither spoke. And then he got to his feet, towering over the bed.

'You'll be safe,' he told her, a raw note charging his tone with dangerous sensuality. 'Dinner will be ready in half an hour. If you'd rather eat here, a tray will be brought in.'

She almost took the coward's way out, but sheer pride lifted her chin. 'I'll be out shortly,' she said, adding with spirit, 'Do I dress?'

'Wear whatever you like,' he said curtly, and walked out of the room.

Heart still thudding in her ears, Leola scrambled out of bed, trying to block out the seconds when Nico's hand had smoothed the skin of her shoulder. His face had been hard, the arrogant features more prominent, the half-closed eyes fierce and demanding.

That intense attraction had been mutual, and the thought both chilled and exhilarated her.

Was this what had torn her parents' marriage apart—this dangerous combination of excitement and hypnotic physical attraction?

Every muscle tense, she recalled her anguished turmoil when her mother had left her husband and twin daughters to follow her lover.

Shivering, Leola splashed cold water over her face. During their adolescence both sisters had kept free of emotional ties, a wariness that had solidified in her when she'd followed her dream into the world of fashion. There she saw enough painful love affairs to decide that life was simpler and more pleasant without passion.

But she'd never met anyone like Nico Magnati before.

Ringing Giselle and talking the situation through would help, but, although she craved a dose of her sister's astringent pragmatism, she didn't. Somehow, for the first time ever, she couldn't share this with Giselle.

But she'd have to ring her in case she was worrying.

She straightened and dried her face, noticing that her sponge bag had been put onto the vanity. By the prince?

The thought of him walking through the room as she lay sleeping made her feel acutely vulnerable.

No, she thought logically, he'd have sent a servant in— she hoped it had been a maid, not the silent manservant.

Despising herself for dithering, she eyed her few clothes. Just as well the prince had told her to wear what she liked, because her wardrobe was basic. In the end she chose a simple silk shift the same tawny hue as her hair, and sandals that made the most of her long legs.

A knock caught her by surprise as she applied lipstick. After composing her face into a pleasant, noncommittal mask, she opened the door.

Nico smiled, his gaze skimming her with appreciation that held nothing of the raw passion she'd seen before. 'Very fitting,' he approved, and offered his arm. 'I hope you won't be bored staying here. Do you like opera?'

'It depends,' she said inadequately, laying her fingers

gingerly on his arm. Trying to ignore the tension that sprang into life inside her, she wondered if he planned to take her to the theatre. Surely not?

She went on, 'If it's something modern and atonal, no. Why?'

'I am trying to find out something of your tastes,' he said gravely.

'I like the classics,' she said, still acutely suspicious. 'And most other music. But you don't have to entertain me.'

He led her into a drawing-room. 'Champagne, I think,' he said, and poured two glasses.

Leola glanced around the room, hoping she wasn't being too obvious in her appraisal. It was much safer than watching her companion, dressed in casual clothes that had clearly been tailored especially for his broad shoulders and narrow hips and those long, heavily muscled legs.

Think furniture, she told herself sternly. This is probably the only time in your life you're going to visit a prince's house.

It was decorated in the same style as her bedroom— modern luxury spiced by pieces that could only have come from Illyria, like the painting of a prince in elaborate sixteenth-century armour. Mounted on a prancing charger, he was posed in front of a large, grim castle.

Leola examined him, then sneaked another glance at his descendant. Yes, there was a definite resemblance, although Nico's cold grey eyes had come from somewhere else in his gene pool.

Of course he caught her, that black brow climbing as she hastily gestured at the picture. 'An ancestor?' she asked.

'Alexander the Fourth, noted for his ferocity in battle and his astuteness. He fell in love with the daughter of the ruling prince of Illyria, but she was promised to a son of the King of France. He kidnapped her.'

Leola accepted the glass he held out, and concentrated hard on setting it down on a small table. 'So it runs in the family. I hope she made his life hell,' she said pleasantly.

His smile was swift and appreciative, and did very strange things to her insides.

'She did,' he said, 'but as she was in love with him too they worked it out. Mind you, he had to give up quite a lot to appease her father. Until then the Lords of the Sea Isles had been more or less independent, although ostensibly they owed fealty to the ruler of Illyria. Alexander had to cede most of his rights to the Prince of Illyria.'

'He must really have loved her,' she said, surprised.

'Of course he did. We Magnati are noted for our very successful marriages.' He raised his glass and finished with an irony that suggested he didn't mean what he was saying, 'To love.'

'To successful marriages.' She sipped the most superb champagne she'd ever tasted.

'You don't believe in love?'

'I believe in it,' she said coolly. 'I just don't think it's necessarily the most important thing in a good marriage.'

'So what is the most necessary quality to achieve that?' he probed.

She shrugged, uncomfortable yet not backing down. 'Shared values, I suppose. And respect—trust. Pleasure in each other's company that's not solely based on physical appetite.' Heat stung her skin. She went to take another sip of champagne, but decided it wouldn't be politic. She didn't know how much sedative was still swirling around her bloodstream.

'Interesting,' he said thoughtfully, 'if perhaps a little prosaic. Are you warning me off?'

If he could be direct, so could she. She lifted her head and gave him a straight look. 'I'm not in the market for any sort of affair.'

His mouth hardened. 'Good, because neither am I. However, to make this work we need to look as though we are very much in lust.'

'I told you before, I'm no actress,' she warned.

He set his glass down before coming across to her. 'I don't think you'll need to act,' he said evenly, and slid his hands around her throat in a gesture that should have been threatening.

Unable to move, to breathe, she stared at him, her gaze darkening when his fingertips swept across the pulse that fluttered in the vulnerable hollow at the base of her throat. The tiny caress summoned a languorous desire, fiery yet honey-sweet, that licked through her body in a slow, feverish tide.

Deep in his eyes she saw the crystalline ice heat, so that they became burnished and opaque, almost impersonal in their unwavering focus.

Terrified, Leola tried to think of something to say, something crisp and pertinent and indignant that would stop this silent, heady seduction. Her brain stayed dumb; lost in the reckless silence, she stiffened when Nico bent his black head and kissed the place his fingers had touched.

His warm mouth lingered across the silken skin, setting off tiny explosions in every cell. Leola dragged in a sharp breath, valiantly fighting the hunger that urged her to yield, to let herself sink against that lean, big body…

And then he released her and stepped back, saying

blandly, 'Fortunately there is enough chemistry between us to convince anyone who is watching that we have indeed found something rare and precious.'

'Who will be watching? I thought I was to stay here out of sight,' she said, her voice uneven as she struggled to control her rioting emotions.

'Tomorrow night we're going to an Illyrian Embassy reception. It will be safe, the perfect place to establish that you are with me.'

He paused, and she felt a sudden urge to lick her lips and swallow.

Coolly, with a calculation that plucked at her already stretched nerves, he finished, 'And that we want each other so much that no one will be surprised when we don't go anywhere else.'

Leola shook her head, trying to clear it of the drugging fumes of desire. In a voice lacking its usual crispness, she said, 'I don't want to go to a party, especially not one at an embassy.'

He smiled, not a nice smile, and said, 'Stop being so stubborn, Leola.'

He said her name like a caress, the syllables slipping off his tongue. Nerves jangling in a dismaying mixture of frustration and arousal, she snapped, 'I don't have anything suitable to wear.'

'You will by tomorrow night,' he told her coolly.

Leola glared at him. The thought of him buying her clothes filled her with distaste, as though he'd be somehow buying *her*. It might be hugely illogical, but she felt so overwhelmed by his power and his authority that she needed to cling to small things to give her the illusion of some independence.

Indicating her silk dress, she said evenly, 'I can wear this.'

Nico's eyes narrowed. 'I'm desolated to have to say that, although it looks wonderful on you, it isn't suitable.'

'I know that,' she returned evenly, 'but I'll have no use for formal party wear once you've decided this supposed danger is over. I could hire something, of course.'

After another of those ice-sharp glances, he enquired, 'Or possibly buy some fabric and whip up something overnight?' His voice hardened. 'There is no need. Someone will come to the house tomorrow with a selection of clothes for you to choose from.'

Fuming, Leola decided that if he was a typical example of the breed, growing up as a prince meant imbibing arrogance with your milk. 'I'd need a little more time to produce anything worth wearing,' she said loftily.

He ignored the comment. 'And unfortunately this danger is not *supposed*. I was told today that questions have been asked on the island about your affair with me.'

An unpleasant chill slithered down her backbone. 'By whom?'

'A contact in San Giusto.' While she digested that he went on with a grim resolution that further unnerved her, 'You can be confident that you are safe here.'

Against all common sense she believed him, although logic told her that no one could be completely protected. Curiosity drove her to ask, 'How do you come to be caught up in this?'

He shrugged, his eyes unreadable. 'Sheer chance.'

A likely story, she thought disbelievingly.

He indicated the door. 'You must be hungry; dinner is ready.'

The meal was served without any oppressive formality, the prince summoning a compelling charm to which Leola succumbed, even though she knew he was deliberately wielding it as a weapon. They talked of books and politics and the latest shocking collapse of a huge industrial conglomeration.

Halfway through the meal she realised she was enjoying matching wits with him.

Yet beneath her cool, sharply defined politeness prowled other emotions, other sensations—heat in the pit of her stomach when he smiled, a sizzling excitement that leapt from cell to cell, threatening to wipe away the years of control and caution, the bleak memories of just how much havoc unbridled passion could bring in its wake.

Fighting her humiliating weakness, she tried to ignore the powerful musculature of his shoulders, and the way his superbly cut trousers hugged those lean muscled thighs as he walked to a bookcase and stretched to reach a volume they were discussing.

Even his voice, deep and measured with that faint hint of an accent, sent shivery thrills through her. Possibly because beneath the inflexible control she discerned an intriguingly rough undernote.

It seemed she was suffering her very first adolescent crush. Too late now to wish she hadn't been quite so scathing when her friends had groaned their hearts out over some manifestly unsuitable male.

Prince Nico of the Sea Isles wasn't a man to take lightly. And it was time to free herself from this web of attraction, she decided, getting to her feet. 'I need to e-mail my sister in New Zealand,' she said. 'Do you have a computer I can use?'

'What will you tell her?'

After a pause she said reluctantly, 'Nothing about being here. She'll only worry.'

Directing another of those keen glances at her, he said, 'I'll get you a laptop.'

It was small and new and smart, and very easy to use. He set it up for her on the desk in her bedroom and left her to dash off an airy note to Giselle about how pretty the Sea Isles had been and how cold the weather now that she was back in London. She didn't mention losing the internship, or that surreal incident in the square in San Giusto and its disturbing, unexpected aftermath.

Or Prince Nico's name, and the danger he said could be lying in wait for her.

Giselle's similarly brief answer the next morning told her that all was well in New Zealand.

Summoned to the prince's study after breakfast, Leola was informed that a security man would be in the house from now on.

Bluntly she asked, 'Do you really think that's necessary?'

'I don't know.' Nico surprised her with his frankness. 'But I believe in hoping for the best and preparing for the worst. I'll introduce him before I leave.' He met her eyes with hard intensity. 'Consult him before you do anything at all, and don't go out of the house.'

'All right.'

She'd seen—and pitied—trophy wives accompanied by security men, and wondered if perhaps those men in their well-cut suits and carefully blank expressions were like harem guards, making sure the pampered, expensively dressed women didn't stray.

Now she was lumbered with one of her very own.

Nico said, 'Do you know Magda Wright?'

Leola said distantly, 'I know *of* her, of course.'

Everyone in fashion knew of Magda Wright, a *grande dame* born of Russian emigrants who'd carved out a career dressing an exclusive clientele in clothes that were a byword for timeless elegance. You didn't choose Magda Wright; she chose you. Word had it she could turn a carthorse into a thoroughbred.

Leola stared at him, her chin lifting. Meeting such a legendary couturier would be a terrific thrill, but she had no intention of letting him buy her any more clothes.

'She was a friend of my mother's,' the prince continued. 'I asked her to bring a selection of clothes this morning for you to choose from.' Before she could answer he finished, 'You'll like her and she'll like you. Don't give her a hard time.'

'I'm never rude,' she said on a steely inflection.

'Only to me.' He grinned, laughter dancing in the grey eyes, and touched the knuckles of one hand against her jaw.

It should have been a threatening gesture, but somehow he turned it into a caress. Leola took a swift, shocked breath as tension shimmered across her nerve ends, a potent pull of attraction she couldn't control.

In a voice totally devoid of expression the prince said, 'I'll see you later.'

Magda Wright was a small, dumpy woman dressed in standard black, with sagacious eyes and an air of cheerful sophistication. Clearly she was intrigued, but the discretion she'd learned from years of dealing with the rich and powerful prevented her from asking questions.

However, she startled Leola by saying, 'Show me your clothes.'

'I—are you sure?'

'Of course I'm sure. No need to bring them down; I'll come up and see them in your room.'

Anticipation hollowed out Leola's stomach. As they were going up the stairs she said, 'I should tell you that I don't plan to choose one of your dresses.'

Magda Wright looked amused. 'Will you also tell me why?'

'Because—' Leola hesitated, then admitted with a wry smile '—because I'm contrary and I'd like to wear something I designed.'

The woman beside her gave her a shrewd glance. 'And you do not wish Prince Nico to pay for your clothes?'

Leola's chin came up. 'Well, yes, that too.'

Amusement glimmered in the other woman's dark eyes. 'I like your style. So you wish to dazzle?'

'If I can.'

'We will see what we can do.'

Magda examined everything carefully, checking the seams and the cut with an expert's eye. Leola found she was holding her breath when finally the woman turned and said, 'I like your designs very much.'

Leola flushed. 'I—thank you.'

'When Nico contacted me he told me a little about you, so being curious I checked you out. I like your sharp, modern edge, yet your clothes are very wearable.' She eyed Leola up and down with the peculiarly analytical gaze common to plastic surgeons and designers, then switched her gaze to the few garments on the rack. 'Out of this lot, which would you choose to wear to this reception?'

Leola hesitated, then admitted, 'I don't know what's suitable for such an occasion, but I like this one.' She indicated an ivory silk shift.

'So, put it on.'

Obediently Leola got into it. The long sleeves and deep

cross-over neckline only hinted at her body beneath, although the skirt—ending halfway between her thighs and her knees—blew discretion out of the window.

'With legs like yours you can get away with that skirt,' Magda observed, nodding. 'What would you choose to wear on them?'

Without hesitation Leola said, 'I've always worn a pair of shimmering tights, and high-heeled sandals in the same colour.'

'Excellent,' Magda approved, nodding. She went across to the cases she'd brought with her and unlocked one. 'Decorous, yet subtly sensuous. Fortunately Nico, unlike so many men, is excellent at description, so I have brought an array of accessories that might suit. He said you were a lion woman, and he was right.'

Leola flushed. 'It's just my name and the hair,' she said uncomfortably.

The older woman chuckled. 'I don't think so. You have that air of unconscious pride—a little subdued right now, but still there.'

Something in her voice deepened Leola's flush. How much did she know of the debacle at Tabitha's? Probably quite a lot; gossip at her untimely departure would have filtered through their small, circumscribed world.

Suddenly serious, the older woman went on, 'Before I saw you I felt I should warn you not to expect too much from this liaison. Men like Prince Nico Magnati like to play with women like us, but when it comes to permanence they choose their own sort.'

'I know that,' Leola said uncomfortably.

'And Nico is—well, it is too unfair to say he is a playboy. He likes women, and when he takes a lover he is faithful and considerate, but there is never any question of marriage, and if the woman looks like she is falling in love with him, he breaks it off before he can cause her too much hurt.'

A fierce, shocking stab of jealousy startled Leola. If only she could say, This is all fake—a charade. I am not his lover—never will be.

Instead she said, 'Thank you for the warning.'

Magda Wright nodded. 'But now that I've met you I know you have pride and ambition and talent, and wisdom enough to know your own value. Just don't fall in love with him.'

Leola could feel colour stealing into her skin, but she met the older woman's wise, seen-everything eyes with frankness. 'I won't. It's all right.'

'I hope so. He's a dangerous man.'

'You mean he breaks hearts?'

Magda Wright paused, then said deliberately, 'That as well.'

CHAPTER FOUR

A SHIVER scudded down Leola's spine. What on earth did the woman mean?

Magda went on quietly, 'His mother Evgeniya was a concert pianist—a superb one. I dressed her for her performances. Her music meant so much to her, though it couldn't save her in the end. She loved her husband beyond adoration, and, although he loved her, exile ate into him like a canker; his sole aim was to return to Illyria and the Sea Isles. When he was murdered she committed suicide.'

Horrified, Leola said, 'I didn't know he was killed.'

'Poisoned on the dictator's orders,' the older woman said succinctly.

Leola felt sick. 'How old was Nico—the prince?' she amended rapidly.

'Only fifteen, a mere boy. He took it very badly. It stole his childhood from him.'

So they had something in common after all. Recalling her own family tragedy, Leola said quietly, 'It's a bad time to lose a parent.'

At least she'd had her father—distant and angry though he'd been—and her sister. And of course there had always been Parirua, the place she'd been born in, the anchor for their family.

Torn between an unusual desire to know more about the prince, and the feeling that to ask came too close to prying, she hesitated.

The older woman looked past her. 'It seems as though your prince has come,' she said as someone knocked on the door.

Leola swung around. 'Come in,' she said, her skin tightening.

When Nico held out his hand she had to force herself to walk across to him, stiffening when he pulled her close for a second before releasing her. Dry-mouthed, she looked down at the hand resting lightly, possessively, on her shoulder, its lean strength a silent signal to the other woman in the room.

'I happened to be passing,' he said, eyes keen beneath his long lashes. 'Are you two ready for lunch?'

It was far too easy for Leola to smile up at him while her heart performed gymnastics in her chest. 'Yes,' she said simply, dicing with danger, consoling herself that she'd be safe with Magda there.

But Magda said regretfully that she had another appointment, one she couldn't miss. Startled by the eager anticipation this news gave her, Leola then retreated behind a cool mask as she and the prince ate. In fact, halfway through the meal when he was called away to take a telephone call she told herself the only thing she felt was relief.

Once he'd left the room she took a deep breath, trying to ease the taut strain on every muscle in her body.

Her reaction to Nico shocked her. It seemed like a sort of treachery. Ever since she'd been able to hold a pair of scissors she'd loved clothes, and as soon as she realised that some people actually made their living designing them she'd been determined to join that select band—no matter what the obstacles.

Now she realised that some of those obstacles could be personal. It would be perilously easy to allow herself to be diverted from her ambitions by his unsettling and danger-ously hypnotic charisma. It humiliated and scared her that she had no control over her own emotions.

No, she corrected herself, *emotions* weren't causing her this turmoil. The powerful, frightening drive that swept her away whenever she saw Nico had nothing to do with her feelings, and everything to do with lust. He'd kindled it when he'd kissed her, his demanding mouth lighting a fire that refused to die.

She'd never felt anything like it before, and she despised herself for not being able to conquer it.

Her emotions were her only weapons. She counted them off—resentment at her total dependence on him and his refusal to tell her what this was all about, distrust, anger at the way he'd ridden roughshod over her needs and fears and caution...

Almost guiltily she started when Nico came back in, his expression remote, and said, 'I'm sorry, but the call was important.'

'I'm sure it was,' she said, her smile tight.

He gave her a keen glance as he sat down. 'Tell me, how did you end up working at Tabitha Grantham's?'

'Hard work and luck.' Well, she'd thought so at the time. And although it had come to a crashing, embarrassing end, she'd learned a lot in the months she'd spent there.

'It must have been a coup for you. How did she know that you had a talent she wanted to exploit?'

'I took a design course at a polytechnic in New Zealand, and after I graduated was offered a job in one of the biggest fashion houses there.'

'Because you're good?'

'Because I'm good,' she agreed without false embarrassment.

'Go on.'

'My employers let me do a sort of mini-collection for New Zealand Fashion Week; Tabitha and her partner were holidaying in New Zealand, so of course they were invited to all the shows.' Infusing a certain distance into her voice, she concentrated on the coffee she was pouring. 'She liked what she saw of mine, and offered me work experience for a year— like an apprenticeship, with her as mentor and the chance to feature if I came up to scratch. My New Zealand employer encouraged me to go because contacts are hugely important for a designer, and the experience would be invaluable.'

'So what happened?'

'We decided we didn't suit,' she said, a challenging note in her words. She handed him his cup, glad of the chance to avoid his too-perceptive eyes as she poured her own coffee.

'Why?'

Heat tingeing her skin, she let her brows drift upwards. 'That's not actually any of your business.'

Something moved in the depth of his eyes. 'The rumour going round is that you and her partner were lovers.'

From between her teeth, Leola said, 'You can tell whoever fed you that bit of information that it's a lie. As if I would sleep with a man old enough to be my father. He makes my flesh crawl.' Her voice dripped contempt.

'He's rich and influential,' Nico said cynically, 'and

you're ambitious. Some people would see that as a combination made in heaven.'

'I'll get where I'm going under my own efforts,' she told him, frost in every word.

'And that's what you want to do for the rest of your life— cater to rich women's whims?'

Indignation overcame her caution. 'It's not that at all— it's the satisfaction of making people look good. And it's not only rich women with whims who want that.' She assessed his jacket and shirt with one swift glance. 'Even you succumb to it. If you didn't, you wouldn't go to Protheroe and Sons for your tailoring—you'd buy your clothes off the peg.'

He gave a short laugh. 'I use them because it's convenient— I'm bigger than most men, and they have my measurements.'

Satisfied, Leola produced a cool, disbelieving smile. 'Of course. If you say so. I love designing, I love the fabrics and the cutting and the excitement of knowing that I'm part of a huge, glamorous industry that also happens to provide employment for thousands of people, as well as make a lot of money.'

Nico's lazy smile set her heart flipping in her chest. 'I believe you,' he drawled. 'I assume you dressed your dolls as a child?'

'Of course, and anything else I could get to stay still long enough. We once had a dog…' She stopped. The impulse to confide in him came too close to intimacy.

'Go on,' he prompted with a lazy smile that sent sexy little shivers across her skin. 'Don't tell me you dressed a dog?'

'Only in covers,' she said primly. Poor little Coco had been her mother's Chihuahua, barely tolerated by their father, and each winter the shivering creature had welcomed the tiny outfits she'd made and decorated for it. 'Not in human clothes.'

When their mother left Coco disappeared—put down, she and Giselle later discovered, by their father.

Soon after Nico left, and Leola sat down at the laptop he'd insisted she use to make notes on embroidery she'd seen on some costumes in a museum in San Giusto, then sketched the motifs, noting the skilful stitching and wild use of colours.

She also succumbed to another nap, wondering when she woke if this was still the results of the drugs she'd been given, or if she was simply exhausted by the happenings of the past few days.

The afternoon dragged, although she spent some time choosing a book from the prince's shelves and then curling up with it. The security man was nowhere in evidence, and towards evening the grave manservant told her that the prince sent his apologies but wouldn't be there in time for dinner. Did she want to eat at the table, or would she prefer a tray in her room before she dressed for the embassy reception?

'A tray, thank you,' she said, angry at her foolish disappointment.

In her room she checked the clothes she planned to wear, and went over Magda Wright's warning in her mind, reinforcing its message. She and Nico had nothing in common. She belonged to the world of fashion, not to the worlds that intersected with it and were served by it: the jet set, the film stars, the world of big business and what Magda called 'society'—with the quote marks emphasised.

Princes might well figure in her future, but only as the husbands or lovers of customers.

OK, so when she thought of Nico her body sprang to life,

eager to experience the untamed, consuming energy she sensed in him, but that meant little.

Presumably it was exactly how her mother had felt when she'd run away with the lover who'd later abandoned her.

'Sex,' she said scornfully to her reflection in the restrained luxury of the bathroom as she went through her skin-care routine. 'That's all it is. Plain, common-or-garden sex. It's potent but it's dangerous, so you'd better get used to ignoring it.'

Nico's powerful physical presence touched something darkly elemental in her, an urgency she'd never suspected she could feel. If she were more experienced—had *any* experience—she might be able to deal with it. Unfortunately she suspected that relaxing her guard for even a second might hurl her into a future as dangerous as it was tantalising.

Because unless he was a superb actor, Nico found her at least mildly attractive. That thought summoned more of those erotic little chills and a twist of heat to her sensitive places.

Attractive enough to actually want her?

'Don't be an idiot,' she told herself firmly, stepping into the shower.

But the thought wouldn't leave her, tempting her to dream. Her severe talking-to about being sensible and practical got hijacked by reckless memories of how Prince Nico looked when those hard grey eyes heated...

'Stop that right now,' she muttered, so scandalised by the vivid images her brain conjured that she turned the cold water full on.

She should be hearing warning sirens, she thought mordantly, shivering as she wrapped herself in her threadbare dressing gown—probably the least attractive robe ever seen in this house. No doubt the prince's gorgeous lovers wore exquisite things of silk and lace for his delectation.

Stifling another humiliating pang of jealousy, she sat down to compose a short e-mail for her sister in New Zealand. She got as far as 'Dear Giselle, how are things?' and stopped, repressing a pang of homesickness.

Life on Parirua station seemed very simple, very true and honest. Oh, Giselle had her problems, but they concerned the weather and cattle and lack of money; she didn't have to deal with the sort of emotional turmoil that was scrambling her twin's thought processes right then.

Hastily Leola wrote a short, innocuous message and sent it off. Things were changing, she thought disconsolately, then lifted her head and squared her shoulders. Giselle had never seemed so distant, New Zealand so far away.

After the solitary dinner she did her hair and make-up, then dressed, examining herself with a super-critical eye. She liked what the ivory silk did to her skin and hair, while the sandals and shimmering gold stockings made the most of her long legs. Magda Wright had even produced a ring, a circlet of tiny diamonds surrounding a gold stone the exact colour of her dress.

'Is it a diamond too?' Leola had asked suspiciously, eyeing the central stone.

The older woman laughed. 'A canary diamond that size would come with its own bodyguard. No, it's just a gold topaz. Pretty and quite valuable, but not serious jewellery.'

Leola glanced at the clock and picked up a wrap and bag. Heartbeat quickening, she walked out of her room and along the hall to the drawing-room.

Magnificent in austere, perfectly tailored black and white

evening clothes, the prince swung around, eyes half closed as he appraised her.

'Magda told me you insisted on wearing your own clothes.'

She stiffened. 'Yes.'

'You were right to do so. You have style,' he said thoughtfully. 'Edgy style, and you can carry it off. You look superb.'

Breathe, dammit. 'Thank you,' she said briskly. 'So do you.' And could have winced. Hardly sophisticated repartee.

Broad shoulders lifted. 'I'm gratified you think so.' He took the evening jacket she carried and held it out for her.

Acutely aware of him, she slid her arms into the sleeves. 'I like Magda,' she blurted, her skin tightening at his closeness.

She waited for him to move away so she could breathe properly.

Instead, he looked down into her upturned face, his eyes cool and measuring. 'Because she understood your reasons for wanting to show off your own clothes?'

'Partly that, but also because she's a nice woman as well as a genius,' she told him, stepping away to give her heart a chance to slow down. She returned the cool scrutiny he'd just subjected her to. 'You're very sensible to stick to completely conventional evening dress. Big men can't get away with frills and exotic touches.'

'I'm relieved I meet with your approval,' he said, his grave tone qualified with dry humour.

Which left her with nothing to say, so she spent the drive to the embassy trying to banish the whisper of fairytale magic with a dose of prosaic common sense.

It didn't work; the whole evening fascinated her. Held by the Illyrian government in a magnificent Georgian building to celebrate the anniversary of the restoration of freedom to the Illyrians, the party was like something out of a novel.

Magnificent clothes were everywhere, and some *very* serious jewellery. Prince Gabe Considine, a cousin of Nico's, hosted it with his wife, and Nico had a kind of roving role; keeping Leola at his side, he made sure no one was neglected or overlooked.

She'd expected to be completely out of her depth, but good manners, she thought ironically, were good manners anywhere.

So it was startling to be faced with overtly bad manners when she met a sleek Englishman who was introduced by Nico as a famous violinist. After a brief, bored greeting the man ignored her to concentrate on trashing an opera he and Nico had both attended.

He also ignored the woman with him, much younger and superbly sophisticated, who spent the first five minutes examining Leola's clothes, hairstyle and ring with unhidden interest.

However, she seized a gap in the conversation to say huskily, 'The tenor is completely miscast.' She bestowed a glance on Nico that held more than a hint of avidity. 'When I think of *Don Giovanni* I always think of you, Your Highness. Handsome as sin, too sexy and rich for his own good, and—like Byron the poet—dangerous to know.'

'You flatter me,' he said with a thin smile. 'I think. Although I don't know that I appreciate being compared to Byron, who behaved like a posturing mountebank with no sense of humour. And my singing is best confined to the bathroom.'

'Perhaps we should ask Ms Foster if she agrees with that,' the woman said, her eyes flicking to Leola's carefully controlled face. 'But we might be boring her. Do they have opera in Australia?'

The subtle hardening of Nico's body against her hurried Leola into speech. 'New Zealanders are very laid-back,' she said with a glittering smile, 'but we do object to being mistaken for Australians. And because I'm a complete philistine when it comes to tenors I'll have to take Prince Nico's voice at his own valuation.'

She smiled up into his face, and caught the glinting, appreciative laughter in his eyes.

A few minutes later they moved on, and he said calmly, 'He was a friend of my mother's—in fact, I suspect that he was in love with her. But now he has arthritis and can no longer play, and it has soured his temperament.'

He didn't mention the musician's companion.

When the evening had wound its way to its finale, Leola sat back into the limousine. The chauffeur and bodyguard were dark silhouettes in the front seat, and the privacy screen was down. Their shoulders touched; it was far too intimate.

Leola broke a silence that was rapidly becoming taut.

'That was an interesting evening.'

'I hope you enjoyed it,' he said courteously. 'I'm sorry you had to deal with Alida Verres' rudeness.'

The ice in his tone startled her. Shrugging, she dismissed the woman. 'I shouldn't have been quite so quick to take offence; I know people have difficulty distinguishing between the Australian accent and ours. And *Don Giovanni* was my mother's favourite opera—she used to play it quite often.'

'So it has memories for you.'

'Yes.'

Something must have shown in her tone because he said, 'Not good ones, perhaps.'

A little harshly she said, 'Not entirely.' And before she

could stop she heard herself explain, 'My mother left everything behind when she went away; the first my twin and I knew of her elopement was when we came home from school to find Dad burning her music. All the operas, all her Edith Piaf CDs—everything went onto a bonfire.'

Perhaps, Leola thought with an unexpected insight, in her music her mother had found some of the passionate drama she'd craved. She'd certainly died like some of its tragic heroines, alone and abandoned and penniless.

She looked down, and saw that she'd been twisting the ring on her finger.

'So we both had mothers who left us too early,' Nico said, his warm fingers closing around hers in a grip as dangerously comforting as it was unexpected.

Her heart seemed to stop, only to suddenly burst into life again, beating with an exhilaration she could almost hear. She didn't dare look at him; the lights of London pulsed on their linked hands, setting off tiny, swiftly vanishing explosions as the yellow topaz caught them.

Nico lifted her hand and kissed it. 'It still makes you sad?' he said as he lowered it.

Stomach clenching, Leola clamped her mouth shut, because she had no intention of telling him that when her mother's lover had taken her to Spain he'd stayed only long enough to help her spend her half-share of her husband's assets.

When she'd gulped enough air into her starving lungs to answer, she muttered, 'A mixture of emotions, actually. Anger because she left us, but, yes, sadness for her too.'

Nico didn't probe, for which she was very thankful. What on earth had possessed her? Fellow-feeling, the conviction that he would understand because he too had lost parents?

If so, she'd better get over it.

'I was angry too when my father was killed,' he said.

A raw note in his tone made her look up sharply. Against a glare of headlights she saw his profile—arrogant, bluntly defined and fiercely uncompromising.

'It must have been dreadful,' she said, then shivered. 'Words are pretty inadequate, aren't they.'

'Unfortunately, yes. We had little money—my father wasn't good with it, and my mother died soon after—but Roman refused to allow me to be taken by relatives.' His mouth curved in a sardonic smile. 'I assume he knew that I would only run away. Fortunately he was able to send me to his old boarding school—I have no idea where he got the money—where they managed to knock off a few of the sharp corners.'

Like her, he wasn't telling the whole truth. Leola wondered why she knew, and thought how extremely odd it was to be sitting beside a prince swapping intimate details of their childhoods, while fierce little chills ran from their linked hands straight to her heart.

'So you had your brother and I had my sister,' she said inanely.

'Does she look like you?'

She seized on this much safer subject. 'As far as features and build go, yes, we're pretty near identical, but she's black-haired and white-skinned, with green eyes.'

'And does she work in fashion too?'

Again she heard an equivocal note in his voice. With reserve she told him, 'She's a farmer.'

'Indeed.'

His tone was an invitation to confide, an invitation she

resisted, instead leaning away from him as if she were fascinated by something on the pavement. He lifted his hand from hers, and she shivered, feeling oddly bereft.

Back at the house he said, 'There is food ready if you'd like a snack before you go to bed.'

She should turn now and go up the stairs and lock her bedroom door behind her. Coward, she thought trenchantly, obeying an irrational recklessness that persuaded her to say, 'I'd like coffee, thank you.'

They drank it in his study. One glance took in the very modern communications set-up on one desk, another the bookshelves lining the walls, and there were flowers and good pictures on the walls.

Back in New Zealand, she knew a room very like this—smaller, furnished less opulently with mainly Victorian pieces, but with the same relaxed, masculine ambience. Her father had spent most of his time in it, almost ignoring his only children in his bitterness and grief.

'Brandy with your coffee?' the prince asked.

'Brandy would be lovely, thank you.'

Nico's attention was caught by her brittle tone. He saw her straighten her shoulders and continue her survey of his study. Something shadowed those sultry gold-sparked eyes, and tightened the lush outline of her mouth.

What was going on beneath that fall of tawny-amber hair, held back tonight so that her face was fully revealed? Although she'd been the ideal companion, assured, calm and socially adept, her emotions had been rigidly controlled, even when confronted with discourtesy and insolence.

He tamped down a cold, determined anger. Alida Verres had never forgiven him for turning her down when she'd made a play for him. Ready to intervene, he'd watched her work herself up to aggression, but Leola had forestalled him, more than able to defend herself against the other woman's attack.

His decision to protect Leola by passing her off as his lover had been the only one left to him once he'd realised that she'd find some way of escaping from Osita; unfortunately, he hadn't realised just how much she'd get to him.

Right now he wished very much for the pretence to be reality.

Although she wasn't classically beautiful, something about her stirred a primal, consuming passion in him. The loose dress was skilfully sexy; just skimming her body to merely hint at the sleek litheness beneath, it made the most of her curves and those superb legs, and she'd used cosmetics to emphasise her eyes more than her lips.

He wanted her. In his bed. And she wanted him; he was too experienced not to read her reluctant response.

But because it *was* reluctant, it wasn't going to happen. Taking her would further complicate an already complicated situation, one he was doing his best to keep the lid on.

He concentrated on pouring a splash of brandy into each of two glasses. 'I hope you like this,' he said austerely.

After a cool look she veiled those amazing eyes with her long lashes. When she raised the glass to her mouth, and sipped delicately he had to look away in case she noticed the bold desire coursing through him.

She was every bit as aware of him as he was of her. And he knew what would happen if he kissed her.

Elemental chaos.

CHAPTER FIVE

DELIBERATELY, Nico put his untouched glass down, then leaned over and relieved her of hers, setting it down beside his.

Leola looked up, heart pumping into overdrive at his predatory stance, the shimmer of ice in his eyes. No, not ice, she thought confusedly. Heat…

He said her name, and although she knew she should run, her muscles locked and all she could do was drown in the darkening intensity of his gaze.

His smile sent an erotic shiver of anticipation down her spine. 'Leola—it's a pretty name. Was there any reason for it?'

Her voice was barely audible. 'My mother said I was born with lion-coloured hair.'

His brows shot up. 'So why did your parents name your sister Giselle?'

'Black hair,' she said on a soft, breathy intonation. 'Think ballerinas, dying for love with smooth blue-black hair pulled back into a bun. Our mother was a romantic.'

Too romantic to survive…

'And what about you?' Nico eased his hand towards the silken skin that tightened as it waited for his touch. 'Are you a romantic too?'

When it came the caress was nothing more than the lightest sweep of a fingertip from beneath her ear to the juncture of her neck and shoulder, yet she felt its effect through every cell, swift as lightning and as powerful.

'Not a bit,' she said huskily, resisting the desperate need that surged into demanding life through her.

How could her voice sound so cool when inside she was quivering? Unconsciously she swayed towards him, eyes slumbrous, skin delicately flushed. With a taut, narrow smile, Nico gathered her in his arms.

She expected to be crushed against him, but he held her loosely, giving her the chance to pull free. 'If this is not what you want, say no now,' he said, his voice deep and sure and confident.

Baffled, she stared at him, longing for his warmth and strength, her nostrils filled with that faint, male scent that had so oddly reassured her in the Sea Isles.

Although he wanted her, he was in complete control. For a second she hated his sexual self-assurance, and resented the women who'd given it to him.

Well, she had very little experience, but she wasn't going to tell him that. 'Why?' she asked, then wondered if he thought she was simply being provocative.

'Because if you wait much longer I might not be able to let you go.'

But he would, she thought bleakly. He sensed and understood the heat coiling through her, the fierce urge to discover where surrender would take them both, yet instinct told her that if she said no he'd let her go.

Such steely self-discipline was a direct challenge, and she had never been the type to run away from a challenge.

Her head came up. She met his narrowed eyes in a glittering counter-attack and said sweetly, 'I meant, why would I want to say no?'

Smiling, he said, 'Are you playing games with me?'

Kiss me, she thought recklessly, but he wasn't going to dazzle her into yielding. His implacable gaze told her silently that they were playing this according to his rules.

The decision was hers.

Leola made up her mind. Challenge or not, dangerous or not, she wanted to explore this reckless hunger a little further.

'I'm not into games.' Fingertips tingling, she raised a hand to outline his mouth.

He caught her forefinger in his teeth and nipped, and when her mouth formed an O of surprise he bent his head and kissed her.

With a muffled groan she let herself relax against him, feeling his body harden instantly. He lifted his head and looked at her for several seconds with burnished, intent eyes, then kissed her again, and there was nothing gentle about this one; he took his fill of her mouth as though he'd been hungering for it for years, tasting her with a carnal enjoyment that sent excitement breaking over her, carrying her off into unknown realms of sensory experience.

Nico Magnati knew exactly how to make a woman feel both cherished and passionately desired. Skilfully he ratcheted up the sensual tempo until she could think of nothing but the next step in this erotic exchange, feel nothing but the divine exhilaration that kept time to the frantic beating of her heart.

He lifted his head, said something in the language she recognised now as Illyrian, the syllables liquid and fierce before he crushed them against her mouth.

His arms tightened around her and she felt the full impact of his arousal. Obvious male ardour had always repelled her before, but now her whole body flamed in wildfire response. To her astonishment she found herself pushing against him, aching with a primal need that demanded satisfaction.

And then he broke the kiss. A feverish shudder tightened her skin; until that moment she'd never understood the clamouring potency of desire.

'So where do we go from here?' he asked, his voice taut.

Almost she had allowed this to happen, let herself drift into surrender. But in spite of the languorous heat of the moment she summoned the will to force up her heavy eyelids and meet narrowed, darkening eyes that glinted with something like cool satisfaction.

It was like a dash of ice-water in her face. Whereas she was almost mindless with passion, Nico was still completely master of his emotions. If she agreed, she'd just be another of his women; it was terrifying to admit, but she wanted much more from him than the casual sating of a casual desire.

She was, she thought with a clutch of panic, in too deep already.

That knowledge gave her enough strength to mutter, 'Nowhere,' and she pulled herself free.

Only to find that with her first instinctive wrench he let his arms fall and with an impassive face stepped backwards.

Just like that, as though it meant nothing.

He said with a humourless smile, 'In that case, it would be a good idea if you took your coffee and brandy with you to your room.'

'I don't think I need either,' she said numbly, and looked around for her evening jacket and bag.

Nico swore silently as his cell phone rang. Brows drawing together, he picked it up, his frown deepening when he heard the voice of the man who controlled security on the Sea Isles. It took an effort to rein in his unruly body and, in a voice deliberately pitched to go no further than the cell phone, say one word, a password that established who he was. The man at the other end replied with the correct answer.

Leola scooped up her jacket and bag and set off for the door.

Watching her straight spine and erect head, Nico demanded in Illyrian, 'What is it?'

'We finally have someone prepared to give evidence.'

'And it will stick?'

The man who'd been his comrade in arms said laconically, 'Backed up by your Miss Foster, I can't see why not.'

Nico swore in a soft, chilling monotone that cut through the silent, luxurious room. He saw Leola stiffen, then hastily open the door.

As it swung closed behind her he said abruptly, 'No.'

'Why not?'

He paused, unwilling to admit that something deep and protective in him wanted Leola kept well away from anything to do with this situation. 'Not unless it's impossible any other way. What other evidence do we have?'

The other man relayed a litany of information gathered with great difficulty, of incidents that had painfully woven a mesh around one of the most important men in Illyria.

When he ran down Nico said curtly, 'I doubt if that's enough to convict Paveli. I wish I'd seen him that night in San Giusto instead of dragging the one witness off to safety.'

'It would have made things much simpler. Of course, there are other ways of dealing with him.' Into the silence that followed his Head of Security said, 'Years ago you used one of them.'

'No.' The word cracked through the opulent room like the flick of a whip. 'Prince Alex is doing his utmost to replace the blood feud with the rule of law. I won't countenance that.'

'You did once. And don't tell me you regret it, because no one else in Illyria does.'

'I do regret it. What you're suggesting would be assassination, pure and simple.'

His employee and friend persisted, 'I agree wholly with our prince, and with you, that the old ways have no place in a modern society, but sometimes, when the evidence is uncertain but the heart and mind are not…'

'No,' Nico said uncompromisingly. 'We live in different—better—times now.'

There was a silence, until his friend asked, 'So, what do you want me to do? Continue keeping Paveli under surveillance, of course, but what else?'

Nico said, 'Are questions still being asked in San Giusto about Miss Foster?'

His friend laughed. 'No, everyone is sure she's your latest lover. Taking her to London and installing her in your house was a brilliant idea. Paveli doesn't seem interested in her any more—if he ever was.'

'Possibly not, but it would be foolish to underestimate him.' Swiftly, he reviewed the available options, and then gave orders.

Then he put the cell phone down and stood with his mind racing furiously, until Leola's face blanked out everything else and he found himself reliving the feel of her in his arms, sleek and graceful.

And willing.

Only for a short time, he thought with a humourless smile.

She'd been right, of course; it was too soon, yet somehow he felt that he'd known her far longer than the few days of their acquaintanceship. He enjoyed talking to her; she never bored him, and, although he was damned sure she wanted him, she'd kept her distance, not even flirting with him.

It intrigued him, the subtle strength, the reserve, the cool self-containment that was both challenge and lure. But then, he found her infinitely fascinating—her husky voice, the faint fragrance that seemed to come from her skin rather than any perfume, and the lush, fulfilled promise of her lips…

Yet he'd detected a certain restraint there, too. Her kisses had been surprisingly innocent. He certainly wouldn't have been the first man she'd kissed, and from his experience the people who worked in her field were pretty casual about sex.

And why the hell was he thinking about her experience— or lack of it—when he should be concentrating on other, infinitely more dangerous problems?

Leola lay taut in her bed, wondering who had called him so late at night. And why.

Not good news, she thought with a shudder. His reaction had shocked her; well, not his *reaction* because she hadn't understood the words, but the tone he'd used still sent shudders through her.

And raised questions—lots of questions.

What was this mysterious business they were caught up in? How dangerous was it? He apparently thought it enough of a problem to go through this farce of a pretend relationship so he could protect her, but until she'd heard him answer that phone the whole situation had seemed so far-fetched she hadn't really believed in it.

Oh, face facts, she told herself ruthlessly. Beneath everything—the indignation, the resistance—she'd secretly rather hoped that he'd brought her here because he felt the same fierce, almost irresistible attraction that was undermining her defences.

Clearly that wasn't so; and now she felt a clutch of panic at the realisation of serious danger.

'No,' the prince said.

Leola's head came up abruptly. 'I beg your pardon?' she said with freezing distinctness and stormy face. 'I don't recall asking your permission.'

'It would not be sensible,' Nico told her impatiently.

'Nonsense.' Leola set down her coffee-cup and stared at him across the breakfast table. 'What can possibly happen to me at a Chanel showing in Paris? Do you have any idea how difficult it is to get tickets for that? The security is so tight that no one will get close to me.' Without giving him time to answer she swept on, 'Your friend Magda Wright thought I might enjoy it, and I will, but that's not the important thing. Contacts are all part of the game here, and it's a huge opportunity for me. I'll be perfectly safe.'

'No,' he said implacably.

She stared at him, eyes glittering with temper. 'No one— no *sane* person—is going to kidnap me, or murder me, or whatever it is you think might happen in a room full of fashionistas and the jet set, not to mention photographers!'

Nico reconsidered his first instinctive refusal. The few

days since he'd kissed her had passed in comparative peace—if it could be called peace when they manoeuvred around each other as tensely as stalking lions, he thought wryly.

'You are, of course, right,' he said, adding, 'However, you could still be attacked on the way to the venue.' He regretted his words as soon as he'd said them, because her face paled.

'Do you really think that might happen?' she asked soberly, her gaze meeting his with level insistence.

No shrinking, no terror, he saw, and admired her courage. 'I don't know,' he admitted. 'Which is why I want you where I know I can keep you safe. But if you feel it's so important to go to Paris, I'll come with you.'

Startled by a sudden leap of delight, Leola felt it seep away into fear. She desperately wanted to snatch this opportunity, because it might be her only chance before she was forced to return to New Zealand, but—what if Nico came and something happened and he was hurt? She'd never forgive herself.

The thought of that beautiful male strength shattered because of her ambition made her feel sick.

'No, it's all right,' she said quickly. 'I'll stay here.' Magda's offer had come as such a surprise, she'd let herself get carried away. Actually, she didn't even have the money to get to Paris.

He shrugged. 'I haven't been to a fashion show before. It will be a new experience.'

'You wouldn't be able to get a ticket,' she argued, thinking how much more she'd enjoy it with him there—and knowing that she was sailing straight into perilous waters indeed.

One black brow lifted in sardonic query. 'Think so?'

A reluctant smile replaced her glower. 'I suppose not. It must be great to be rich and influential!'

He grinned. 'Don't knock it. I've been poor and without prospects, and I prefer this.'

'Who wouldn't?' she said honestly, before curiosity drove her to ask, 'When were you poor?'

'When I was a child. My mother earned an excellent income, but neither she nor my father were good with money. When they died we had nothing. Roman worked damned hard to get us on our feet. I owe him everything.'

Leola looked at him, shivering a little when she recalled the telephone conversation he'd had after he'd kissed her. He'd gone from being would-be lover to formidable man of action in an instant, and she'd recognised the attributes that made him so successful—iron-hard ruthlessness, forceful authority, unsparing toughness.

And a brilliantly incisive brain, she knew from her research on the internet. His brother might have helped him at first, but Nico would have succeeded.

On a hunch, she asked, 'Did you do time in the army?'

'Yes,' he said, and without any alteration in his tone went on, 'So when do you plan to go?'

'Are you sure?' Torn, she suggested, 'You'll probably be bored.'

He shrugged. 'Surrounded by exquisite models? I doubt it.'

A pang of jealousy—fierce and elemental—pierced her. Repressing it, she gave him the date.

'All right, leave it to me.' He made a note. 'My PA will make the arrangements.'

Seated once more in the same private jet that had transferred them from Illyria to London, Leola thought again that in many ways life was much simpler if you were rich and influential.

Except that she'd seen now how hard Nico worked; he could take time off when he wanted to, but he spent long hours either at the office or in his study, running the huge enterprise that made up his and his brother's empire.

And there was this other business, the one that she'd somehow found herself mixed up in...

'You're frowning,' he said with a searching glance. 'What is it?'

'Nothing.' She made a small grimace. 'Actually, I'm hoping that my wardrobe is suitable. Did I tell you Magda went through it with a fine-tooth comb?'

'Somehow, I'm not surprised. Was there a tussle of wills?' Although Magda was noted for her autocratic behaviour, he'd back Leola when it came to making her own decisions.

'A couple,' she admitted, smiling a little ruefully. 'She thought I might be veering too close to punk in some of the things I wanted to take.'

'So?'

'So they're in my case,' she said cheerfully. 'I'm only getting one chance to impress the French. I thought I might as well give it a go, and she agreed in the end, because actually I don't do punk. I have my own style.' She flashed him a slightly taunting glance. 'I hope it suits the image you want to project.'

'I don't care about image,' he said dryly.

'You tried to insist on me wearing one of Magda's dresses to the embassy reception instead of my own.'

He shrugged. 'I wanted you to feel comfortable, and I knew the other women there would be wearing their best.' His smile was ironic, but his eyes were amused. 'Had I known you better I'd have not tried to pull rank—as well as being an extremely talented designer, you're more than capable of dealing with anything that comes your way.'

'Thank you. I think.'

Of course he didn't care about his image. Not only did he have a personality and character that made an uncompromising impact, but he dressed with such assurance—and he had a gorgeous body to drape clothes on.

Hastily she banished her feverish imaginings. One day, she thought, she might take on the tailors—have a go at putting out a men's range...

As if he'd read her mind he asked idly, 'What are your plans for your future?'

His question pulled her back from a serious case of back-sliding; she'd just remembered how he'd felt against her—lean and hard and potent—and her pulses were jangled erratically. Reminding herself of the stunning beauty of his mistresses—discovered on another guilty excursion on the internet—she told him, 'My employers in New Zealand are keeping my job for me, but it won't be too long before I go out on my own.'

'An expensive procedure, surely?'

Leola repressed a qualm. 'Not if I'm sensible about it—and if I can convince a bank that I'm to be trusted with their money.'

He frowned. 'You have no other family but your sister?'

'Oh, a collection of cousins on my mother's side, but I have no intention of borrowing off them. My father was an only child. Why?'

'Just that you seem very alone.'

'Twins are never alone,' she told him.

'Can she help you with your plans?'

'No.' Giselle was struggling with an almost bankrupt

cattle station; she'd be more than eager to help if she had any spare cash, but there was none. Leola said lightly, 'I can make it on my own. Plenty of people have.'

'I admire your spirit and your confidence.'

A glance at him revealed that he was serious. Leola looked away, feeling an uneasy heat along the sweep of her cheekbones. 'Good things both, but it's talent and persistence that will get me where I want to go,' she said. 'And at the moment I'm just thrilled to be going to Paris. When I was a kid I used to pore over my mother's fashion magazines and pretend that I was a Parisienne; I really thought that everyone in France dressed like the models in the photographs.'

He laughed, as she'd meant him to. 'I hope you're not too tragically disillusioned.'

'I won't be.'

And she wasn't. They stayed in an apartment there—joined, she was surprised to find, by Nico's older brother. Prince Roman Magnati was gorgeous in an entirely different way from Nico, although both were tall and dark and charismatic.

She liked him, she discovered, and he was courteous and pleasant to her.

As he could only spare twenty-four hours, Nico swept her off for a quick tour of the city highlights, ending with a breathtaking trip up the Eiffel Tower with Paris spread out beneath them.

'Truly enchanting,' she breathed, turning to him.

He looked down at her, and something in his eyes stilled her laughter. He lifted her hand to his mouth. 'Indeed,' he said deeply.

The kiss burned on her skin even after he let her go and turned to point out the Arc de Triomphe.

Several hours later she examined herself minutely in the mirror. She'd anguished for hours over what to wear, finally choosing a silk dress geometrically printed in subtle shades of amber and gold and bronze. She emphasised its high boat neckline and short sleeves with bronze leather gloves that finished above her elbows, and its short skirt with tights and boots in the same colour. She'd dressed her hair simply, just pulling it back from her face and holding it with a bronze clip.

'Yes, you look pretty good,' she said, trying to hide a pang of apprehension.

The show was superb. And Nico had also got tickets for the party that followed, held in a huge warehouse miraculously transformed into a pavilion of pleasure. When he decided it was time to leave the party and go home, Leola was floating on a high.

She'd been introduced to two film stars, and had her photograph taken, when she was standing beside Nico's brother. Refusing to let it go to her head, she'd done her best to network, helped by Nico's presence at her side.

He'd known what she was doing, of course, even helped her. Magda Wright had warned her that in Paris she'd be ignored, that she'd be there on sufferance, the lowliest of the low. Instead, at Nico's side, she'd been ushered into the front row, handed one of the 'star' goody bags, treated like the royalty he was.

The film stars and the elegant fashionistas, the superbly groomed and dressed society women who fluttered smiles and eyelashes at him, recognised him—as did their men— and she was intrigued to see that everyone treated him with great respect.

Obviously they too recognised that forceful aura of authority.

Yet, although she'd been hugely impressed by the show, having Nico beside her meant she couldn't fully concentrate on it.

She sat up straighter, staring sightlessly through the window. He was invading her mind, she thought worriedly; when he wasn't with her she thought about him constantly. OK, he was utterly gorgeous, but her absorption in him had to be because she was so dependent on him—living in his house, eating meals with him, his remembered kisses burning through her defences whenever she relaxed her guard.

Naturally she was overwhelmed. A girl from a cattle station in Northland in New Zealand sitting beside a prince in Paris, staying with his brother who had the evocative, centuries-old title of Lord of the Sea Isles of Illyria, and meeting people whose names she'd only ever read in magazines and newspapers.

Possibly threatened by an unknown someone for reasons beyond her knowledge.

Definitely in danger of feeling too much for the man sitting a few inches away in the back of the big limousine purring through the streets of Paris. Something ominously like panic hollowed out her stomach.

'Tired?' Nico asked.

'A little,' she admitted. 'It was—exactly what I expected, only more.'

'More?'

'More everything,' she said soberly.

'Every famous designer was once in the same position as you.' His tone was crisp and assured, a little off-putting.

She nodded, feeling rebuffed.

'What is it?' Nico asked.

'Nothing.' She hoped her voice was bright, not brittle. 'I'm realising how much I have to learn.'

'I refuse to believe that you're daunted,' he said thoughtfully. 'What's caused this?'

She gesticulated at the interior of the car, at the streets with their elegant, wafer-thin women, at the ancient buildings. 'Everything feels too much like a fairy tale.'

And Prince Charming was beside her, his long legs stretched out, his shoulders blocking a fair portion of the streetscape, his eyes uncomfortably penetrating. Her heart gave a huge leap, then dropped.

Oh, damn! she wailed silently. This is serious.

Not love. It couldn't be love. In spite of the days spent living with him, she didn't know Nico well enough to feel anything more than gratitude that he took his responsibilities so seriously.

Gratitude, and lust, she admitted reluctantly. But then, her forays into the world of internet research had told her that very few women didn't succumb to his potent male impact. She'd discovered that his liaisons were conducted discreetly and usually lasted no longer than a year or so.

So this elemental wildfire excitement wasn't love. Which was just as well, because how could she possibly tame a playboy prince? He'd always chosen experienced women for his lovers; the sum total of her experience was a few kisses and some mild groping she'd endured with distaste. The only time she'd ever enjoyed a man's caresses was when he'd kissed her, but she didn't have the skills to keep him intrigued for a month, let alone a year.

However…instinct told her that Nico would be a truly stupendous first lover. It also warned that she might very well be burnt badly if she followed this train of thought to a conclusion that had been hovering at the edges of her mind ever since their gazes had first clashed.

A sideways glance from beneath her lashes revealed that he was watching her, his face half alien with the play of light and shadow over his angular features. Her heart gave another huge jump in her chest, and the sizzle of awareness that kept her alert and taut whenever he was near intensified into an urgent, driving energy.

After swallowing surreptitiously to ease her dry throat, she said, 'I'm not daunted. I suppose I just feel a long way from home.'

His hand closed around hers. Electricity rioted through her, but as well as fierce excitement his grip offered comfort and strength.

She could get to rely on it, she thought, and the prospect was so terrifying she jerked her hand free. 'But I was determined to make the most of it and I had a wonderful time,' she told him.

'I was impressed at the way you worked the room,' he said thoughtfully.

'With your help.' She gave him a direct glance. 'No one would have come near me if you hadn't been there.'

He smiled narrowly at her. 'A title is useful for attracting social climbers,' he drawled, 'but it's different in the real world of business. There you have to earn respect. You should make it.'

CHAPTER SIX

NICO contemplated his companion in silence. To his surprise she asked suddenly, 'Are you still sure there's a chance someone recognised me that night in San Giusto?'

'A chance only.' It would be foolish to accept that a cunning fox like Paveli would accept the masquerade for truth, but it did seem likely.

He allowed that hidden possessiveness a little more rein, smiling down at her as she turned from her scrutiny of the streets. Her smoky eyes, shadowed in the darkness of the car, met his fearlessly.

'I wish you'd tell me what it's all about.'

'It's safer that you don't know.'

'In your opinion,' she returned smartly.

His voice hardened. 'And that of several others I trust, including Roman.'

After a moment's hesitation, she nodded gravely. 'I've never thanked you for offering me your protection, but I am grateful. Even if it's not actually necessary,' she added, and fixed him with another considering stare. 'Have you any idea how long this—this *charade*—is likely to go on?'

'Until enough evidence is gathered to bring the ringleaders to justice.'

'I asked you before how you got tangled up in this, but you refused to tell me. I think you owe me some sort of answer.'

'Anything that happens in the Sea Isles is my concern,' he said coolly.

He wondered what was going on behind her perfectly made-up face. Did she sense the same currents between them, the rapidly building tension that had caused him too many restless nights, and the headstrong craving that was eating away at his gut?

'In other words,' she said crisply, '*noblesse oblige*? Because your ancestors were better tacticians—and more ruthless—than their opponents in any power struggle, they became the ruling lords in the Sea Isles, and because of that you owe it to the people you rule to take care of them?'

'Exactly.'

'Don't you think that's a bit outmoded in the twenty-first century? Almost patronising?'

'Spare me a lecture on democratic rights, if that's what you're about to deliver.' His smile didn't take the sting out of his words, but he moderated it in his next comment. 'If the dictator hadn't taken over, the Illyrians would have come to democracy the same way as other countries did, but they were denied that process.'

She flashed him an indignant look, firming her delicious mouth before saying sedately, 'I wasn't going to lecture. I don't know enough about Illyria to give an opinion on it, but although I was only there for a few days I saw the poverty. Something has to be done. I just wondered if the people know better than you do what they need.'

'Of course they do. That's what we—the old aristocracy, if you like—are trying to do. Persuade the people that the rule of law is better than the ancient system of blood feuds, that they have the right to insist on making their own decisions. They need time to recuperate, to learn to take freedom for granted, before they can work out their own destiny.'

He wondered how he'd become embroiled in this discussion, when all he wanted to do was kiss the words from her delectable mouth.

He was not in the habit of discussing his obligations with his mistresses. Except that she wasn't his mistress. And even if they started an affair she'd always be her own person, never just a beautiful possession, eye candy for others to ogle, a splendid body to take pleasure in.

But then, he didn't care for trophy women, chosen to impress. He'd always picked lovers with care and discretion, enjoying their company as well as desiring them. Though he'd made sure they understood the rules; he didn't like hurting people, so whenever any showed signs of wanting to deepen the relationship he'd ended the affair, sometimes reluctantly.

Because he had no intention of marrying, not now and not in the future. One act of madness had proved he was no fit mate for any woman, no fit father. If heirs were needed for the Sea Isles, then Roman would have to provide them.

'We're working on the poverty,' he said, 'but it's taking time. The islanders are slowly getting used to the idea that their input is necessary if they're to get what they truly want. Throwing off the repression of all those years is difficult for them.'

They talked about his and his brother's plans for the

islands until they reached the apartment. Inside the opulent drawing-room she eased her fingers free of her long gloves. 'Does Roman live here?'

'No. He and I do a lot of business in this part of Europe so it's useful to keep an apartment here. We both call the Isles home; Roman is on his way back there now. He had an urgent call around lunchtime.'

Leola said, 'Oh.' Heat burned through her skin at his gaze. Hastily she finished removing the gloves and put them down on a side table. 'I see,' she finished lamely.

'It makes a difference?'

She resented that poker face he assumed on occasion. He wasn't one for openly displaying his feelings, but it hurt her in some obscure, never-to-be-examined way when she couldn't discern them at all. 'No, of course not.'

In London they shared a house, so why the jittery excitement? Expectation hummed through her, and this time she couldn't resist it. It was part of the magic of Paris, an inevitable progression of her own feelings, that tonight she should make an important decision in any woman's life—to take her first lover.

It was time, she thought. It didn't matter that he didn't love her; she wasn't like her mother, longing for a romantic passion that a devoted husband couldn't provide. She'd faced and accepted that there was no long-term future in an affair with Nico, so she'd be safe.

Or as safe as any woman could be around Nico.

The thought filled her with a heady exultation, barely tempered by a very real fear.

Of course he might not be interested.

Even as the sly suggestion formed in her brain she

rejected it. He wanted her; all she had to do was show him—without being obvious or crass—that she wanted him too.

Easier said than done. Watching him pour a small amount of cognac into two balloon glasses, Leola wished she had some knowledge, some basic seduction techniques that would help her here.

Everything that came to mind seemed impossibly fake. She had no tricks, no lures or flirtatious techniques. Well, she'd always been frank with him; should she just say, Nico, let's go to bed together?

The thought made her cringe. She gulped down too much brandy; it burned down her throat, making her cough. Oh, *hell*, she thought as tears started to her eyes, how very sophisticated!

'Here,' he said, laughter deepening his voice, and turned her face to meet his.

Hot with embarrassment, Leola clamped her eyes shut, flinching when he wiped away the tear from one eye with a gentle finger.

'I have a better idea,' he murmured.

As she waited in silent humiliation for him to fish out his handkerchief she felt his arms come lightly across her back, and a kiss touched each eyelid.

Her heart blocked her mouth; she couldn't breathe, couldn't do anything but freeze.

Nico removed the glass from her shaking fingers; she heard the soft clink as he set it down. She didn't move, even though she knew she must look utterly stupid standing there with her eyes shut.

'Look at me,' he said. And when she refused, he commanded quietly, 'Leola, look at me.'

Hugely reluctant, she lifted her lashes, and met an amused

grey survey—until the fine-grained skin darkened over its magnificent framework and his eyes narrowed.

'Why?' she managed to croak.

Without her even trying, that innocent choke had set everything in motion. Exultation roared through her, and fear, backed by a yearning hunger.

'So you know who I am,' he said coolly. 'A woman should always know who she's kissing.'

And his arms tightened around her, his body hardening against her as his mouth took hers with a bold deliberation that shocked her as much as it pleasured her.

His previous kisses had stimulated and excited her; this frankly erotic one plundered without mercy, demanding that she meet and match it. Helplessly, no longer concerned about anything but this reckless passion, she opened her mouth to him, yielding her mind and her body, letting him know her as no one else ever had.

Her wholehearted surrender must have surprised him because he gave a soft grunt, and pulled her into the cradle of his hips.

A violent shudder of need shocked her.

His eyes gleamed as they met her dilated ones. 'That dress has been tantalising me all evening; I've been hoping you'd give me the privilege of taking it off,' he said tautly. 'Did you wear it for me?'

Of course she had. Without even realising it—making up and spraying herself with a sexy, taunting perfume…

All for Nico. 'Yes.'

He bent his head and kissed her throat before running his hand up her arm. The slightly roughened tips of his fingers on her skin made her catch her breath.

He said, 'Too much too soon?'

'Oh, no,' she said without thinking, her pulse rioting when he cupped her breast. *Not enough*, her brain whispered hungrily.

Not nearly enough...

Need exploded in her, travelling in a desperate surge from the warm caress of his hand to every cell in her body. When a whimper broke from her he stopped the sound with another kiss, this time filled with carnal intention.

He lifted his head and looked around the room as though he'd never seen it before. 'Not here,' he said harshly.

'No,' she agreed, although she didn't care. Dazed, her senses rioting, she realised with a total lack of embarrassment that if he'd wanted to take her on the sofa she'd have willingly let him.

'In your room.' He slid both hands into the hair she'd so carefully caught back, releasing the strands so that they fell around her bemused face in a warm, tawny flood. His fingers moved across her scalp in a measured, drugging caress that sent tiny excited shivers down her spine, adding to the storm-clamour of turmoil in her body.

'I—yes.' Her eyes enormous and very blue in her hot face, she muttered, 'But I'm not protected.'

'I'll do that,' he said and kissed her again, this time swiftly, and left her at the door of her bedroom.

Once inside, Leola stopped and stared around her. Driven by unsatisfied desire and a fiercely primal anticipation, she couldn't wait passively for him, but what could she do? Clean her teeth? Shower very quickly?

She couldn't even pull the blankets back because someone had already done that. So she strode across to the dressing table and began to take off the earrings she'd worn—a pair of art deco ones she'd found in a market in Auckland.

Only to have her fingers clench around one as a shimmer of movement in the mirror heralded Nico's arrival. Her breath coming quickly through her lips, she watched him walk across the room; it had seemed big when she was shown into it, but he dominated it without effort, his dark masculinity a dramatic foil to the gilded furniture and silk drapes.

Clearly he was used to this, and completely unfazed at the prospect of making love.

Leola wished she were.

He'd taken off his coat and tie, and presumably he had the contraceptives in a trouser pocket. Silently, he came to a stop a few inches behind her, locking eyes in the mirror.

Colour stung her cheekbones. He didn't turn her around to face him; instead, his hands closed around her upper arms while he kissed the place where her neck joined her shoulders.

Shivering, shocked by the sultry droop of her eyelids, the hungry curve of her lips and the swift resurgence of hunger deep inside, she turned, saying huskily, 'That's—embarrassing.'

'I find it very arousing,' he said, his smile taut and intent. 'In fact, I find just being near you very arousing. It's been a while for you, hasn't it?'

Tell him *now*, the last remnants of her common sense urged her.

So that he could decide he didn't want a woman who had no idea what she was doing?

In a muted voice she said, 'No. I mean, yes.' Oh, hell!

But he laughed and said, 'I know how you feel.'

With gentle ruthlessness he cupped her chin and lifted her

face to meet his mouth, and after that she didn't care about anything except the consuming pleasure his caresses coaxed in her. Skilfully, in between kisses that stole her soul, he undressed her, letting the dress fall to the floor.

Leola stood uncertainly on her high-heeled boots, the tights sheening her legs with bronze, the importunate tips of her breasts peaking beneath the soft silk of her bra.

He said something in Illyrian, his voice raw and thick, then changed to English. 'You unman me.'

Stunned, she let her gaze drop. Her voice unsteady and slow, she said, 'It doesn't look like it.'

'I dare not touch you, or I'll take you without the finesse you deserve.'

His hands strayed to his shirt, and with one strong movement he ripped it open, then shrugged out of it. Eyes widening endlessly, Leola's eyes devoured his tanned torso, her bones melting until she was forced to pull off her boots to keep her balance as he abandoned the rest of his clothes with a lithe grace that burned right through her.

He was—*glorious*.

A bronze god, sleekly honed and muscled, the male triangle of his chest and broad shoulders sloping to narrow waist and hips.

Leola dragged in a sharp breath. He was very, very aroused. Was this going to be possible?

He must have seen her startled glance because he said quietly, 'It's going to be all right.'

In the heated safety of his arms, surrounded by his potent male scent, his mouth on hers, she could believe that everything would be all right. Somehow he managed to undo her bra, releasing her breasts against the pattern of hair across his chest, its friction intolerably stimulating against their sensitised tips.

He eased her back onto the cool sheets, and came down beside her, holding himself in such rigid control that she almost said, Don't worry, I won't break.

But she might.

For the first time she wished she'd given in to at least one of the men who'd tried to get her into bed over the years. Then she'd know what to expect, not be worrying about whether Nico might find her total inexperience boring and unsatisfactory.

Yet although tension set her quivering, her whole body waited eagerly for his possession.

Nico said in a low, harsh tone, 'You are so beautiful—strong and lithe like the lioness your clever mother named you for.'

He kissed one breast, and then the tip, taking it into his mouth as explosive, voluptuous sensations drove everything from her mind but Nico, and her unfettered response to his mouth and his hands, to the whole dynamic, compellingly masculine package that was the man she desired so fiercely she could barely breathe.

When he transferred his attention to the other breast, the intensity of her reaction became too insistent to be borne. Without volition she arched off the bed, demanding something she didn't recognise.

'Not yet,' he murmured, his tone a promise, easing down the strap of her silk bra. 'First, this pretty thing has to go.'

She stiffened slightly, but his mouth followed his hands, exploring the little dent in her flat stomach, the curve of her hips, the satiny skin of the inside of her thighs as the tights and the brief scrap of silk underneath were tenderly, erotically removed until at last she lay bare before him, skin flushed, eyes wild, mouth tender from his kisses, body insistently demanding the next step in this perilous, ecstatic journey.

'Nico, please,' she whispered in a desperate plea for something—anything to ease the piercing pleasure that racked her.

'Soon,' he soothed, but his kiss hurled her further into that passionate, reckless place where all that mattered was Nico.

She clutched at him, her fingers slipping across the smooth skin and powerful muscles; he was sweating, she realised with a tiny shock, and realised too that her touch had sent him over some hidden boundary.

He said something in Illyrian, swiftly translating it. 'Be careful—I am not so fully in control as I'd like to be.'

And he turned and sat up, hastily putting on a sheath.

Leola lay with weighted lashes, her heart thudding as the muscles beneath his olive skin flowed and flexed. And then he came back to her, and the slow seduction began again, until she was panting and desperate.

Only then did he slide his fingers down, smiling with primal satisfaction when the involuntary jerk of her hips gave away her hunger. 'Yes,' he said in a raw, driven voice, 'you are ready, my sweet one, my eager lioness...'

He moved over her, filling her world, his eyes no longer ice-cold but hot, his mouth imprinted by her kisses as hers was by his, his body taut and sleek and strong and potent.

Leola's breath blocked her throat; she shuddered as he carefully eased himself into her. She thought, It's too much, and heard the words as she said them, a choked, sensuous growl.

'Yes,' he said, and when she clamped her legs around him in an instinctive attempt to hold him, he thrust hard and fast.

Leola cried out, her voice broken and joyful, filled by him, her body arching up to meet him, muscles she'd never known she possessed tightening around him.

He said something, but the roar of her blood in her ears drowned out his words, and then their bodies melded, establishing an elemental rhythm, and together they met and separated, gave and took, until waves erupted from her innermost core, spreading out to match the rhythm of their mating, waves that overwhelmed her. All she could do was look into his savage eyes and let herself be carried by that untamed need into some region where nothing else mattered.

In the end she was thrown into release, and held there until he joined her in white-hot fulfilment, head flung back, face dark and drawn as he too reached that overwhelming rapture with her.

Locked in his arms, his big body lax and heavy, she came down slowly, slowly, letting the waves recede into something like oblivion. Tiredness drugged her, weighting her bones and her eyelids.

Until Nico said quietly, 'You should have told me.'

Leola froze. 'What?'

He rolled to one side, taking her with him, one arm holding her clamped to his side while his free hand lifted her chin. His eyes were no longer hot and burnished; she shivered at their cool translucence.

'That this was the first time for you.'

Colouring up, she didn't try to deny it. 'How did you know?'

He shrugged, cloaking that intent survey with his lashes. 'I wondered. There was a certain hesitation—a kind of shyness that intrigued me, because you're not shy. But when we joined, I knew. Did I hurt you?'

'No,' she said, astonished. 'If you knew that this was the first for me, you must have noticed that I had...' *A wonderful time* seemed utterly crass; hastily she chose a different phrase '...that it was wonderful. You didn't hurt me.'

'I'm glad.'

But something about his tone made her awkward. And the poker face was back, shutting her out.

After a second's pause she said, 'I'm sorry if it wasn't what you expected. Perhaps I should have told you, but it's rather hard to drop casually into the conversation.'

His chest lifted and his arm tightened around her. Glancing up sharply, she was relieved to see that he was laughing.

He said, 'I understand that. However, I could have been more gentle.'

'I didn't want you to be gentle! I grew up on a farm—I'm not some fragile flower to be nurtured and cosseted and protected.'

'I understand that too,' he said with obvious enjoyment. 'Very well, then, I will tell you the real source of my chagrin. It is that I had hoped for a long night of pleasure together, and because this is your first time that is not possible. Or even desirable.'

Pink-cheeked, Leola digested this. 'What do you mean—desirable?'

'You're probably a little sore already,' he said with disarming frankness. 'Any more love-making will make it worse.'

'Oh.' Leola flushed more deeply, disappointment chilling her even though he was right. 'That's very considerate of you.'

'It's only fair,' he said, abruptly sobering. 'Any man worth calling a man is considerate with a woman, especially when making love to her. Yes, you grew up on a farm, but you are still less strong than most men. We men are simple creatures; we need to protect those who are weaker than ourselves.'

Simple? she thought incredulously, wondering if he really believed that.

Or expected her to believe it. Some men were easy to read, yes, but he wasn't; he was a complex, fascinating character.

And she, heaven help her, still wanted him.

When he smiled, her heart contracted, squeezing into a hard ball in her chest so that it was difficult to breathe.

'It flatters our feeling of self-worth,' he said, kissing the spot in her throat where a pulse beat erratically. Automatically her hand reached for the warm, damp silk of his hair, holding him there.

Against her heartbeat he murmured, 'And with that, of course, goes the desire to care for those who depend on us.'

'But I don't depend on you,' she pointed out, because it had to be said.

He laughed softly. 'I phrased it wrongly. Your independence is one of the things I find so appealing about you.'

The initial pleasure his words gave her faded swiftly. Did he mean that he wanted her because she wouldn't cling, because she had a life to live? His previous lovers had all been women with professional lives in various fields. Was that what he looked for in them—independence, so that when he cut the connection they had something to fall back on?

She shivered.

He was watching her, his handsome face unreadable. Forbidding her fingers to trace the curve of his lower lip she said sturdily, 'I don't plan to depend on any man, ever.'

It wasn't safe. Her mother had done that, and look where

that had ended—in an overdose alone in a squalid hotel room a world away from the children and husband she'd abandoned.

Nico said, 'Wise woman.'

And without warning he bent his head to kiss her, his mouth warm and sensuous and infinitely persuasive. It wiped every thought from her brain as her body, so newly sensitised to passion, responded in a white heat.

When he lifted his head he said with a crooked smile, 'Perhaps I can show you some other ways desire can be satisfied.'

CHAPTER SEVEN

LEOLA woke the next morning alone in the bed, so exhausted she could barely lift her head from the pillows to check the time. With a sigh she closed her eyes again. The sheets beside her were still warm, which meant presumably Nico had only just left.

Mouth curving in sleepy, sated pleasure, she let her mind drift back into the night.

Oh, he'd shown her, all right. He'd adored her body with subtle mastery, never taking her out of her comfort zone yet hurtling her several times into that ineffable realm where nothing mattered but her response to his love-making, her soaring, shattering release, her complete surrender to the moment. Using his mouth and his hands and the startling strength of his big body he'd coaxed from her an ecstasy that still half terrified her.

And whenever she'd caressed him, when she'd sunk her teeth into his sleek hide at one climax, and moaned in unbidden, noisy delight at another, he'd reacted with a masterful primal intensity that never overstepped the bounds into brutality.

She hadn't known her body was capable of so much sensation. He'd made her feel both wild and cherished, bold and bemused, fierce with demand and piercingly subjugated.

In fact, Nico had shown her new facets of herself. Always she'd been passionate about her career; now, she had to face the fact that she could be equally passionate about a man.

She lay quietly, letting that knowledge seep into her brain, cooling the torrid memories of the night before.

Could she deal with this?

Yes, she thought with painfully acute insight, even though something fundamental in her had changed. Last night she'd been arrogantly certain she could cope with—even enjoy— an affair of no-holds-barred passion. Now she wasn't so sure.

Perhaps she'd inherited something of her mother's helpless yearning for romance, because already the thought of saying goodbye to Nico and never seeing him again had the power to hurt.

So—did she play coward and run? Or take everything she could from this headstrong, outrageous desire, sate it, and eventually bid it a graceful goodbye with courage and a mutual respect?

In other words, she thought, climbing out of the bed to walk across to the window, was she stronger than her mother, better able to deal with any disillusion that might come her way?

She pulled the silk drape back and stood staring blindly at the skyline of Paris, the most romantic of springtime cities.

Yes, she thought sombrely, she was both stronger and more pragmatic. Unlike her mother, she didn't believe this was the love of a lifetime. Nico didn't love her and she didn't love him, so she wasn't expecting the impossible happy-ever-after that had lured her mother to her early death.

Whatever happened, she would always have her career.

And if she got hurt—well, she wasn't fragile. Other people recovered from a broken heart—she could too.

But it would never come to that. She wouldn't let it.

Twenty minutes later, showered and dressed, hair pulled back from her face in a sleek, no-nonsense bun, she applied cosmetics, then braced herself and walked out of the bedroom.

Nico was sitting at a table in the sunlight, reading the newspaper. He obviously hadn't heard her come in, and for a moment she watched him, her heart contracting. The sun gilded his angular profile, emphasising the deep olive of his skin, the slashing cheekbones and the unyielding tilt of his chin.

A dangerous man, she thought warily, feeling her body stir, the slow pulse of sated longing giving way to an ardent response.

And then he looked up and saw her, and in his eyes she read amusement and a kind of tenderness that made her heart sing.

Brightly inane, she said, 'Good morning.'

'Good morning.' He got to his feet.

She didn't know what to say, so she stumbled over her next words. 'I thought I'd better get ready to go, since we're leaving before lunch.'

'Very sensible,' he approved, and bent to kiss her.

Temptation surged, savage and urgent, but he let her go almost immediately to examine her face, his own giving nothing away. Leola's heartbeat picked up speed, frantic traitor to that pragmatic part of her that sensed breakers ahead.

'I wish we could stay a few more days, but it's impossible,' he said with a wry smile, and indicated the open newspaper.

Automatically she glanced down at the page. And

stopped, eyes narrowing, because the person in the photograph was oddly, menacingly familiar. A cold finger traced the length of her spine.

'This—this is the man I saw outside the church in San Giusto—just before you grabbed me,' she said.

'You're sure?' All warmth was gone from Nico's tone, leaving only an incisive authority.

'Absolutely.' Shivering, she scanned the fleshily handsome countenance. He had a mean, thin mouth, and something in his eyes made her shiver.

She scanned the caption, wishing she could read French. 'What exactly does this say?'

'That he's the Illyrian minister for Foreign Affairs.' Nico's voice was almost indifferent.

Her gaze flew to his face. In spite of that neutral tone he looked coldly formidable. 'That's bad,' she said on an indrawn breath.

Nico took the newspaper from her and said, 'For Illyria, yes, but not for you. He's just been arrested and is now in custody.'

Stunned, Leola tried to gauge the emotions behind his crystalline, unreadable eyes. Did he mean—was he going to tell her that she was free to go?

Had she so badly read the situation? A sick panic roiled beneath her ribs and she had to consciously breathe. Surely he'd not just used her for casual gratification?

Slowly, feeling her way, she asked, 'Am I allowed now to know who and what this is about?'

'I think you probably are.'

But he didn't start straight away, merely stood frowning down at her as though mentally censoring what he was going to say.

Eventually he said abruptly, 'You have heard of smuggling people from one country to another?'

Leola blinked. 'Yes, of course.' One of the sewing workshops used by Tabitha had been closed down when it was discovered the women working there had no papers and were being paid practically nothing.

'It is a very profitable business run by murderers and thieves,' Nico said uncompromisingly, that intriguingly faint accent colouring his voice and making him seem almost alien. 'One such criminal organisation has been using the Sea Isles as a staging point for smuggling people from Eastern Europe to Britain and France. Some of the refugees were tradesmen, but mainly they were women.'

Startled, she scanned his stony, ruthless face.

'Women who thought they were coming to legitimate jobs but were instead sent to brothels or sweatshops and treated as slaves,' he elaborated.

'I see,' she said, feeling sick.

'I came into this when it was discovered that the organisation was headed by an Illyrian.'

She looked at him with swift comprehension. 'The Foreign Minister?'

'It wasn't known who, except that he had to have excellent links to the government.'

'That must…hurt,' she said quietly.

He shrugged. 'The years under the dictator forced Illyrians to forget the rule of law. They did whatever they had to in order to survive. Most greeted Prince Alex's return with joy, but some saw freedom as the chance to expand their criminality.'

'How did this man—' she glanced down at the newspaper '—this Paveli, reach such a position of responsibility?'

'With cunning, treachery and murder.' He paused before adding with lethal deliberation, 'He was in the dictator's secret police, and as soon as Paulo Considine died Paveli made sure that anyone who could testify against him was eliminated. In the turmoil after the dictator's death it wasn't difficult.'

'Did *he* kill Considine?' she asked.

'No.' Nico turned away. In a tone that revealed nothing, he went on, 'Very few people know how the man who made Illyria his own private torture chamber died.'

'Do you?' Then she remembered the death by poisoning of his father. Afraid she'd hurt him by her careless comment, she added, 'Painfully, I hope.'

'I believe it was quick,' he said distantly. 'Paveli grew up in San Giusto and he was using the crypt in the church as a transfer station. His presence there linked him irrefutably to the crypt—he could not afford to be seen there. One of his lookouts reported that someone had been in the square that night. Questions were asked, but when he discovered that you were with me he assumed what everyone else thought— that we were having an affair. A reputation as a playboy can come in useful.'

Still in that flat, lethal tone he added, 'He is a rapist, a torturer and a murderer, which is why I wanted you kept safe. If he'd found you he'd have extracted what information he could have from you in case you were not just a tourist and then killed you.'

She went white, and he caught her by the upper arms. More than anything she longed to let herself sink against him, but she stiffened and pulled back.

'I'm all right,' she said in a muted voice. 'I—it was just

a shock.' A deep breath gave her enough oxygen to say, 'I'm afraid I didn't take the situation seriously enough.'

Because she'd instinctively trusted Nico to protect her.

'Perhaps not, but it is over now.'

'I—thank you,' she said awkwardly. She'd shared the most intimate encounters with this man, knew his body almost as well as her own, yet thanking him for taking her to his house, for protecting her from a danger that iced her blood, had her fumbling for words.

She ploughed on. 'You've been very kind—'

'Leola.'

His voice cut her off and she stared at him. 'What?'

'I'm needed back in the Sea Isles. There will be unrest there—the people are loyal to their own, and Paveli has family connections as well as criminal ones. I want you to remain in my house in London for at least a month.'

It's not the end, she thought desperately. I'll still see him—nothing has really changed.

But she knew something had; for the first time she understood the depth of his loyalty to the small principality he called home. If any of his previous mistresses had had a rival, she thought with a flash of insight, it was the Sea Isles and Illyria, not another woman.

Heart clamping painfully, she asked, 'Why do you want me to stay?'

Eyes narrowing, he smiled, yet there was an edge of steel beneath the courtesy when he said, 'This is not the time to proclaim your independence. By supposedly making you my mistress I was able to protect you, but it was a double-edged sword. Paveli is in custody, but it's by no means certain that everyone in his organisation has been caught, and he has made threats.' He shrugged. 'I still feel that the only way to protect you was to do as I did, but it also endangered you. Put bluntly, at the moment you'd be useful as a bargaining piece. I'd rather you stayed under my protection until that possible danger is over too.'

Leola drew in a sharp breath. 'Do you think it's likely?'

They locked eyes until Nico said, 'I don't know, but I would feel happier if you let me take care of you at least until we're sure there is no danger.' His mouth twisted. 'After all, you've been nothing more than an innocent bystander caught up in matters that mean nothing to you. I owe you protection.'

Thoughts and emotions tumbled through her brain. What about us? she wanted to cry. What about last night? But she couldn't ask, and because it would ease his fears if she did this for him, she surrendered.

'You owe me nothing,' she said, forcing herself to sound relaxed and in command. 'Very well, I'll stay for a month, or until you think it's safe. Whichever comes first.'

Hard, ice-grey eyes held hers for a moment, then Nico nodded, and glanced at his watch. 'Breakfast will be ready by now. We'll eat, and then we'll get going.'

Leola sat down, staring around her tiny flat. It had been a rotten day, she thought wearily.

In fact, it had been a bleak two months. She'd barely seen Nico since the day he'd brought her back from Paris.

Three weeks later he'd appeared to tell her that the danger was over; Paveli's organisation had been completely dismantled, and she was safe. He then asked politely and without any discernible embarrassment whether she was pregnant.

'No,' she'd yelped.

'I'm glad to hear that,' he said courteously, his gaze flinty and intent. 'I hope you're enjoying your internship with Magda?'

'Very much.' Greatly damaging her pride, she went on, 'Thank you for organising it.'

'Did she tell you I did?' he asked sharply.

'No, I guessed.'

His voice revealed a cynical amusement that hurt. 'I'm glad you didn't refuse it.'

'I don't do grand gestures,' she said with brittle composure. Women who were penniless and homeless in London had very few options.

He'd shrugged. 'I'm afraid I have to go back immediately. Take care.'

She'd nodded, and watched him go with a stony face.

It had been only sex, she'd thought savagely, abandoning the hope that had kept her company since he'd left. Magnificent, wonderful sex—but it was clearly over and she had to accept that. So she set herself to working even harder for the woman who'd taken her on to please Nico.

Only to discover that neither common sense nor ambition consoled her; she missed him with a bitter, aching sense of loss that showed no signs of abating.

Damn the man, how could he have imprinted himself on her so vividly that she dreamed of him, night after night? She hadn't expected it to hurt so much—but she'd survive this, she thought fiercely.

And then, while she was still settling into the routines of Magda's business, intense turmoil had erupted in her sister's life, ending in the forced sale of Parirua, the cattle station that had been the family base for generations.

Wearily, Leola got to her feet and started to prepare dinner.

Although she loved Parirua it didn't mean as much to her as it did to her sister, but she'd felt Giselle's anguish as though it were her own.

And it seemed cruelly harsh of fate that the buyer should be Roman Magnati, Nico's brother. Talk about malignant destiny, or preposterous coincidences or the sardonic whim of the gods, she thought wearily.

As though the thought had summoned it, the telephone rang. Smiling into it, she said, 'Hello, Giselle.'

'Hello, Leola.'

Leola's antennae sprang into full alert. 'What's happened? You sound happy.'

Her sister laughed. 'I am.'

'You're in love!'

'How did you guess?'

'Oh, come on now, it has to be love—a week ago you were utterly miserable, but now you're happy. What else could it be?'

'I'm not just happy, I'm *very* happy,' Giselle told her as though she couldn't believe her own words. 'In fact, better than happy!'

Leola could hear her sister's smile in her tone. 'Radiant? So who is it?'

Her twin hesitated, then said, 'Lollie—'

Leola shrieked, 'Don't you dare use that nickname! Tell me who he is. Do I know him?'

'Yes. Yes, you do.'

Something in Giselle's voice lifted every hair on her head. 'So who is it?' she demanded.

'Roman Magnati.'

Leola swallowed. *Nico's brother?* 'Roman,' she said in a stunned voice. 'How—?' She stopped, and commanded, 'OK, start from the beginning.'

And while Giselle was telling her how wonderful Roman was, Leola realised that things had changed for ever between them; even though they were still so closely linked that they could sense each other's emotions across the world, she was aware that Giselle was holding a lot back.

And that's how it should be, Leola thought with a pang. Giselle had Roman now.

Aloud she said, 'I'm so glad for you, Ellie. Be very, very happy. Were you going to ask me to design a wedding dress for you?'

'Of course I am!'

'Great. I'll send you some sketches.'

'No frills,' her sister commanded. 'And some clothes, please, for parties and receptions? Roman said your boss—Magda Someone—will know what to send.'

'I'll choose them myself,' Leola promised, still stunned.

'You're a darling,' her practical sister said, sounding slightly harried. 'Roman and I are going to Illyria in a fortnight so I can meet Prince Alex and Princess Ianthe, as well as his other cousins. And his brother Nico will be there too. I think they're planning an official engagement party in the capital, and then we're flying to the Sea Isles for more jollifications.'

It was a measure of her twin's happiness, Leola thought wonderingly, that Giselle didn't seem worried at all by the prospect of a whole royal family preparing to welcome her.

Giselle finished by saying, 'Anyway, he suggested that you come down to stay with us in what sounds like a ghost-infested castle.'

Not Osita? Of course not, Leola thought, angry with herself. San Giusto was Nico's inheritance, along with all the southern archipelago; Roman ruled from the city of San Marco in the northern archipelago.

Leola swallowed again. Grim practicality told her she'd have to cope with seeing Nico again—soon he was going to be family.

'I can deal with ghosts,' she told her sister sturdily.

Including the ghost of an affair that had finished before it even started.

Illyria's capital, a red-roofed city on the shores of a large lake, boasted a castle where its prince and princess lived and entertained. A benign moon shone down on grim stone walls and turrets, softening the burden of the ages for the family party that celebrated the latest engagement in the extended royal family.

Nico hadn't come.

'He'll arrive tonight,' Giselle had told her that afternoon. 'There was some sort of demonstration in San Giusto this morning, and he felt he should stay until things were calm again.'

Instantly alarmed, Leola asked sharply, 'What happened?'

Brows raised, Giselle eyed her keenly. 'Everything's fine. That man Paveli has quite a following amongst the islanders; the jury retired yesterday so they marched as a show of support for him, but Roman said they weren't violent.'

However, Nico still wasn't there, and it was almost midnight. Leola slipped out onto the terrace, letting a tense breath out into the warm Mediterranean air. In the salon behind her conversation flowed and buzzed, laughter and talk mixed. If she turned her head she'd see her sister, magnificent in a stunning ruby dress that made the most of her lithe, athletic figure, her engagement ring catching the light as she moved.

Beside Giselle stood the man she was to marry, Prince Roman Magnati, Lord of the Sea Isles, and talking to them both were the ruler of Illyria, Prince Alex and his wife, Princess Ianthe.

A smile warmed Leola; it was wonderful to feel her twin's radiant happiness, the complete confidence she had in her lover, the trust that flowed between them. For a treacherous second she found herself wondering whether there could possibly be some hope for her and Nico...

No. He'd made that obvious. She looked out over the walls to the lake shimmering in the moonlight, her nostrils picking up the mingled perfumes from the gardens around the palace.

It had been a hectic few days, haunted by paparazzi. Leola had flown in with clothes for Giselle, sternly resolved to show Nico—everyone she met—that she was fine, her whole life on track, a confident professional woman moving into a successful future.

Security was strict. This betrothal—widely touted as the Cinderella story of the year—had come at a time when there wasn't much to keep the world's press busy, except for the trial of the man who'd not so long ago been a minister in the prince's government.

There were photographs and newspaper posters everywhere, so it would be a relief to leave the Illyrian capital for San Marco. Roman didn't expect Leola and Giselle to stay in his ghost-ridden castle; instead, mindful of the proprieties, they were to be housed in a smaller Romanesque house on the coast.

'At least it's no longer got its Romanesque plumbing,' he'd informed Leola wryly when she'd exclaimed with delight at the thought of it.

And he and Giselle had exchanged a look in which laughter and desire were intermingled.

Remembering, Leola stirred uneasily, clenching her hands on the balustrade, still warm from the sun. She was so happy for both of them—and she did *not* feel excluded...

A faint whisper of movement caught her eye. She froze, staring intently into the shadows of the gardens. Had a photographer infiltrated the grounds? Or was this something to do with the obviously volatile situation in the southern archipelago of the Sea Isles?

Memories of the night in the square at San Giusto chilled her blood. Hardly daring to breathe, she eased back into the shade of the huge Phoenix palm at the top of the stone flight of stairs that led from the garden to the terrace and narrowed her eyes to scan the shadows. They coalesced into the form of a man clad in evening clothes. Leopard-dappled by moonlight beneath the trees, he strolled noiselessly towards her—dangerous, almost sinister in the silent garden. Her breath locked in her throat.

She'd known this meeting was inevitable—had been waiting tensely for it to happen.

'Hello, Leola,' Nico said coolly, stopping below the terrace to look up, his face revealed by the moon.

His brother was all Mediterranean, a darkly handsome Adonis; Nico meanwhile had inherited his mother's sweeping Slavic cheekbones and angular, boldly chiselled features. Both men radiated a forbidding impression of force and power, but beneath Nico's cool self-containment there was something raw and fiercely uncompromising, something that made Leola wonder what he'd be like if he ever lost control.

Frightening, she thought with an inward shiver. He'd retained that formidable discipline even when they'd made love…

She swallowed and said, 'Hello.' Her voice sounded a little hoarse, so she tried again. 'Did you fall from the sky, or scale the walls?'

His smile held more than a hint of mockery. 'Nothing so theatrical. I came in through a postern gate and followed the path.'

'I hope you plan to tell Prince Alex that there's a gap in his defences.' Yes, that sounded better—crisp and composed; no sign of her hammering heart or the sunburst of excitement inside her.

'Security is well aware I've arrived. Are you pleased to see me?'

She returned the smile with interest, hoping its brightness blinded him. 'Of course,' she purred, letting a slight tinge of puzzlement appear in her tone. 'Are you coming up, or do you plan to spend the rest of the night in the garden?'

'What do you think?' He began to stride up the splendid flight of steps.

Her reluctant eyes followed the easy deliberation of his gait, the broad, powerfully muscled shoulders that tapered into a narrow waist and hips. She'd forgotten how tall he was.

The old description 'sex on a stick' popped into her mind and was hastily banished. Over two months ago she'd succumbed to the temptation Nico Magnati offered, only to be shown how little her surrender had meant to him.

She had a vocation, a career and a life, and she wasn't going to be swayed from it by a man who made love like some twenty-first-century Casanova.

'So how have things been for you these past weeks?' he enquired, fixing her with an ice-grey scrutiny.

'Hectic,' she said cheerfully, squelching the quiver of response that zinged through her. 'As soon as it became generally known that I was designing Giselle's wedding dress and trousseau Magda was inundated with enquiries, and quite a few turned into orders, for which I undeservedly got the credit.'

Only last week she'd had to listen to one of his discarded mistresses detail his superb skill as a lover—in bed and out—while Leola supervised a few final alterations to her wedding gown. It had been a grisly experience, especially as the soon-to-be bride clearly mourned the loss of Prince Nico's amazing expertise and stamina, not to mention his inventiveness.

'You'll be happy, then.'

His sardonic tone made her feel like some insignificant creature impaled on a pin. She met it with a slight lift to her chin. 'Of course,' she said politely.

His gaze travelled past her to the salon behind her. 'Is that stunning red concoction Giselle's wearing one of your designs?'

'Yes.' After years spent running a New Zealand farm in jeans and working clothes, her sister was determined not to let Roman down. She'd even confided that she was finding the whole process more interesting than she'd expected.

Nico nodded. 'You have unbounded talent. But you know that already.'

'Thank you,' she said calmly, trying to squelch a very suspect flicker of pleasure at the compliment. Talent was good, but just as important were useful things like stubbornness and the ability to work hard, and independence.

Nico let his gaze run over the smooth curves of her shoulders and the curves of her breasts beneath the turquoise silk. There was something arresting about her—something more than the spectacular blue-green eyes, and a mouth that hinted at the fulfilment of any secret desire.

That very determined chin and jawline...

He'd hoped to be able to look at her without any appetite; instead he felt hunger stir and stretch like some untamed beast inside him.

In the room behind the terrace her sister laughed, and looked up at Roman with her heart in her eyes. Nico was rapidly learning to respect his brother's bride, even though she looked so like her twin he wondered why he didn't feel the compelling goad of physical hunger that had assailed him when he'd first set eyes on Leola.

A quirk in his make-up; for some reason he just preferred lionesses to moon women...

But like a lioness, this one was dangerous. She summoned futile desires—a hunger for some sort of commitment, a warmth that melted the coldness inside him. Experience had taught him that he had only himself to rely on, and, although Paveli was in prison, the demonstration that morning showed that the criminal still had power.

As he smiled at Leola, Nico reminded himself that it would be dangerous to let anyone get too close.

CHAPTER EIGHT

RESISTING memories with all the force of his relentless will, Nico said thoughtfully, 'You told me once that some caprice of genetics gave you and your sister identical features and form, but entirely different colouring. Now that I've seen you both, it's amazing how alike and yet how different you are.'

Leola's laughter sharpened the goad of desire. 'I've always been glad we weren't truly identical. We never wanted to be, even though our mother did the twins thing, dressing us the same until we were old enough to insist on choosing our own clothes.'

'I can understand the need to seek your own identity,' Nico said. 'For some years I alternated between trying very hard to be like Roman, and doing my best to be his opposite in every possible way.'

Startled, Leola glanced up.

He knew what she was thinking. 'Adolescence isn't easy for anyone.'

A hard note in the words sharpened her attention. She could see him, she thought—poised on the cusp of childhood and manhood, grieving for his parents, aware that the man who'd ordered his father's death was still alive, and sent away by the brother who was working all hours of the day and night to forge some sort of future for them both.

He must have been lonely in his good boarding school, forced to rely on himself.

Perhaps that explained his iron control, and the aura of danger that crackled around him like unseen lightning.

Perhaps; more likely it was because when she was with him she felt as though she were being dragged willy-nilly into a seductive furnace, hot with the promise of reckless sensuality.

But Nico hadn't been gripped by overwhelming need, she thought grimly. He'd seen an attractive woman and decided she'd make a pleasant playmate; when circumstances had changed he'd shrugged those broad shoulders and moved on without a second thought.

Apart from her, his lovers had all conformed to a pattern: they were sophisticated, beautiful, and experienced, which probably said something about his character, although she wasn't sure exactly what.

Perhaps that the women in his life were for decoration and recreation only? So why had he made an exception for her? Because she was available? The cynical thought depressed her.

And she hadn't really been his lover, she thought with tough pragmatism—merely a one-night stand.

Unfortunately, that one night had left her so acutely aware of him that when her gaze slid over his black and white evening clothes she saw the man beneath, lithe and powerful. Her fingertips tingled when she recalled the sweep of tanned skin, smooth and supple above the hard coiled muscles, and although he wasn't close enough for her to be conscious of that faint personal scent, her heart was already beating faster and heat was collecting in all the secret places of her body.

Ironing out any inflections in her tone, she asked, 'And which did you choose in the end—to be as like Roman as possible, or as different as possible?'

'What do you think?' he drawled.

'I think you probably chose to be yourself.'

He said calmly, 'Right.'

Another silence, too tense with memories. Resolutely she dragged the conversation in a different direction. 'I've been admiring the view. I didn't realise the lake here was so huge.'

'Bigger than your Lake Taupo,' he said, surprising her by his reference to New Zealand's largest lake. 'Although not caused by a volcanic eruption like Taupo. Here an earthquake shook a mountain down to block the river.'

'It's very beautiful—it reminds me a little of Osita.'

'Does it?' He turned and surveyed the waters of the lake, a shimmering band of satin beneath the triumphant moon. 'The mainland is lusher, more traditionally picturesque than the Sea Isles, but I think the Isles breed tougher people. Resistance to the dictator was especially violent there.'

'What could drive a man to such cruelty?' she asked.

A quick shrug of broad shoulders. 'Fear,' Nico stated dispassionately. 'He knew he had no right to be where he was, that if he showed any softness at all he'd be ousted and made to pay for the huge suffering he caused.'

'Yet it was all for nothing. He died, and Prince Alex was made ruler.'

He swung around. 'Your sister seems to be looking for you,' he said coolly, and offered her his arm.

Guiltily Leola turned towards the candlelit room behind, and, indeed, Giselle was glancing out onto the terrace.

Something was worrying her. So Leola smiled up into Nico's dark face and said brightly, 'So she is. Let's go in.'

But walking into the crowded salon on his arm, watching heads turn, feminine eyes glitter with appreciation, people exchange knowing smiles, was sheer hell.

Later, perched on Giselle's bed in the palatial bedroom, she heard her sister say, 'How is Nico?'

'Fine, as far as I could tell,' Leola said brightly. 'What does he *do* exactly? Apart from being a world-famous lover, of course.' An undertone of bitterness in the final sentence surprised her and alerted Giselle, who looked at her with raised brows.

Watch your tongue, Leola told herself angrily. The last thing she wanted to do was spoil this time of radiant happiness for her sister. So she added with a smile, 'I *do* understand he's head honcho of the family business. What I don't know is what the family business is.'

'It seems the Magnati have got interests in almost everything. And Nico inherited huge holdings in the southern archipelago, where you spent your holiday, although Roman says they're more of a drain on Nico's finances than anything. Not that that will worry him; he's a financial genius with a real talent for spotting future trends, and he's already kick-started the islands' economy.'

She looked at her sister and added, 'As for the world-famous lover bit—well, who believes gossip, especially tabloid gossip?' She laughed, the confident laughter of one who knew she was loved. 'At one stage I was pretty certain that you and Roman had had an affair—just because you were photographed beside him at some Parisian fashion show!'

Leola hoped her sister didn't recognise the ironic note in

her voice. 'Never a chance of that. Like him lots, and, yep, he's stunning, but there just isn't that sizzle. Whereas when you two look at each other—wow!'

Her twin said earnestly, 'It happened just like that, too. Even when I was disliking him intensely, I wanted him in a quite outrageous way. I kept telling myself it was just sex—'

'*Just* sex?'

'Well, you know what I mean,' her sister said, her gaze unexpectedly keen.

Images of that night in Paris flashed boldly into Leola's mind. 'Yes, I suppose I do.' And before Giselle could probe she hurried on, 'Are you going to be happy living in Illyria?'

Giselle examined her engagement ring, a fire diamond of such intensity it burned on her finger. 'Yes,' she said without a shadow of doubt. 'I have to learn the language, of course, but once I can speak it reasonably fluently I hope to be of some use. And I love him.'

Clearly in her world there was only one male. Ignoring a vicious stab of envy, Leola said, 'Nico finds our resemblance and differences intriguing, but what interests me is that Roman, whose name is Russian, looks like some Mediterranean god, whereas Nico, with the Mediterranean name, is all Slavic cheekbones and steely threat.'

'Is that how you see him? Perhaps it's his army training—he spent a few years there in something like the SAS.'

Feeling foolishly over-dramatic, Leola backtracked. 'He just seems to exude a sort of—' she hesitated, searching for the right words, then went on slowly '—tough, ruthless authority.'

'Is that what's stopping you from getting together?' When Leola stared at her Giselle said with a shrug and a smile,

'You talk of sizzle—well, that's what I see whenever you and Nico look at each other.'

Leola frowned, steadying her thoughts. 'I've worked hard to get where I am now, and in five years' time I'm going to be on my way to the top. It might be a frivolous vocation, but it's *my* vocation.' She glanced at her sister. 'It's also a career that's pretty hard to combine with any sort of long-term relationship.'

'So what is it about Nico that makes you think you might be tempted into one?'

Leola stared at her. 'I'm *not* tempted!'

'Oh, pull the other one. Look at it logically—what do you have to lose? From a practical angle it would do your career a huge amount of good to be his lover for a while. Think of the publicity.'

'I won't prostitute myself for my career,' Leola told her with hauteur.

Giselle said mercilessly, 'It's only prostitution if you don't want him. But you do.'

Goaded, Leola asked sharply, 'Since when did you become an expert on the battle between the sexes?'

Her sister grinned. 'Since I realised there was one. And don't try to avoid the question.'

'Oh, well, yes, of course I want him. I mean, what's not to want?' Leola tried for flippancy. 'He's fabulous-looking and sexy, rich, and he's a prince. He's also totally and completely in control of himself and his life.'

'And what woman wouldn't want the challenge of breaking that down?'

'Not me!' Leola said fervently. 'No and no and no again. I'm not into taming anything more formidable than bolts of cloth and stroppy customers. But as well as all those good things, he's also a serial monogamist. Surely you're not trying to persuade me to embark on a crazy liaison that's bound to end in tears?'

'Of course I'm not! But you're going to be at a huge disadvantage if you don't accept how you feel about him. Trust me—I've been there and done that.'

'So you're also an expert on relationships now, are you?' Leola said acidly, fighting back a swift surge of heat at her sister's blunt words.

'I'm an expert on you. You want him, and he wants you. And that's all I intend to say about it.' She drew in a deep breath and glanced around her luxurious room. 'Sometimes I feel I'm living in a fairy tale,' she confessed. 'I mean—I've got a maid. And a social secretary. It scares me, because I don't know what Roman sees in me to compensate for the fact that I have no idea how to behave or what to do or even what he expects from me.'

Leola got up and went across to hug her. 'He expects exactly what he's got,' she said vigorously. 'A lover for life and a companion he trusts and respects, a woman who's intelligent and warm-hearted and sensible and strong. I didn't realise until I actually went to the Sea Isles just how tough things are there. Oh, it's beautiful, and the beaches are as fabulous as ours, but the poverty is horrendous! Those little vineyards—a few square metres of soil with stones piled up around each vine—and the hovels the people live in, the total lack of any education above primary levels… You and Roman and Nico will spend the rest of your lives working for them. But you'll be fine. It's a real help that you're experienced in farming and agriculture, and that you've got vast experience on living on the smell of an oily rag!'

Her sister returned the hug. 'Thanks,' she said, her voice shaky before she firmed it enough to say, 'Well, I hope the people learn to like me. I've got these months before the wedding to convince them I'm all right.'

'They'll love you,' Leola assured her.

As she got ready for bed she thought of her sister's confident assertion.

You want him, and he wants you.

That forbidden hunger clamoured into life deep inside her. Yes, she admitted reluctantly, I do still want Nico.

Even before she'd recognised him coming noiselessly towards her through the darkened garden her body had responded with a surge of reckless appetite, a primitive honing of her senses so that her sight was keener, her nostrils more alert to the scents of the night, and her skin tightening as though awaiting a lover's caress.

As the plane descended towards San Marco, Leola examined the grim grey castle on the hill above the white city, rather glad they weren't to stay there.

To her astonishment the drive to their villa on the coast was along roads packed with people, all shouting and waving, throwing flowers and cheering.

She and Nico had been ushered into the same elderly dowager of a car, open to the warm, flower-scented air. Seated in the back, she looked at the vehicle ahead, a much newer one that carried Giselle and Roman, and murmured, 'Roman's people seem to be delighted their lord's getting married.'

Nico nodded, smiling at a toothless old woman who threw him a red rose. He said something in Illyrian that made everyone around roar with laughter and cheer.

Clearly he was popular. A tiny fear she'd not realised she harboured faded into insignificance. Whatever the demonstration had been about the previous day, it didn't look as though Nico was in any danger.

That evening they attended a reception at the castle and met the local dignitaries, and applauded a group of dancers dressed in costumes made exquisite by handmade lace, quite different from that of the southern isles, Leola noted. The drive back to the villa was accompanied by fireworks exploding in the dark, star-glittery sky.

Leola strolled down to the breakfast table the next morning, rather glad that she and Giselle were alone in the villa. 'What's on today?'

'Nothing for you, unless you want to swim in the pool. A language lesson for me in an hour's time.'

Swimming didn't appeal, so Leola wandered into the gardens, admiring the blooms and looking up at the pine-forested hills, so different from the thick, jungle-green of the rainforest in New Zealand.

She felt Nico before she heard him; he came from behind her, and she had to stop herself from whirling around. The sky suddenly seemed bluer, the breeze more fragrant, and that pulsing, forbidden excitement churned her stomach.

'Hello,' she said, not turning.

'I had a tutor who could do that.' Nico's voice was amused. 'I thought he had eyes in the back of his head.'

She kept her eyes on a seat beneath a huge pine, obviously put there so that strollers could sit and enjoy the view—the blue, blue sea, the cypress-clad cliffs, the tall tower with its witch's hat keeping watch over the villa. 'A handy trick for a teacher, I'd imagine.'

'Very useful.' He moved to stand a few feet away. 'I assume it was self-preservation on his part. How do you do it?'

Quite truthfully, she said, 'I have excellent hearing.'

'It must be good indeed to tell you not only that someone is approaching, but who it is.'

Chagrined, she noted the gleam of mockery in his cool grey eyes. 'Well, *hello* is a pretty neutral sort of greeting; it doesn't actually imply recognition.'

His lashes drooped, then lifted to reveal a limpid gaze that was subtly formidable. 'Of course,' he said silkily, and held her eyes for just a second too long before gesturing at the seat. 'Shall we sit down? You look a little pale; although it's not so hot as it will be later in the day, you might need to acclimatise to it.'

He took her elbow with a casual air of possessiveness, as though it was a gesture without meaning, and guided her towards the seat.

The light touch of his fingers on her bare skin sent a series of shuddering, sensuous shocks through her. Expecting him to sit beside her, Leola braced herself, but instead Nico propped one leg up on the seat and looked down at her from a position of authority, his tanned, hard-honed features disciplined and completely self-contained.

Was it a mask? No, she thought, and wondered how she knew that the world only saw what he wanted it to see.

She suspected that not even his lovers understood the man. The woman who'd told her about his prowess in bed hadn't mentioned anything about emotions; apparently she'd been content with his expertise.

Colour heated Leola's cheekbones. Resolutely steering her mind away from that dangerous direction, she said inanely, 'Northland is notorious for its humidity. I'm finding this dry heat very pleasant.'

'It's been a while since you've lived in Northland, yet you still call it home.'

'I suppose you always call the place you grew up in home,' she said, shrugging.

'I don't. Switzerland was good to us, but the Sea Isles are my home.'

'I understand that,' she said thoughtfully. 'Fosters haven't been living at Parirua for anywhere near as long as you Magnati have been Lords of the Sea Isles, but the connection is still strong. And as Giselle and Roman plan to build at Parirua, it's always going to be a home place to their children too.'

She wished he'd sit down; even his close proximity would be marginally safer than having him towering over her like this. She felt crowded, dominated.

He asked, 'What did you think about Roman's plans to turn your ancestral home into a farm park with twenty-three houses on it?'

'I didn't mind too much,' she said promptly. 'I left Parirua when I was eighteen, and although I love it I was never involved in running it like Giselle. Things change; you just have to get on with life.'

'A pragmatic philosophy worthy of you,' he drawled, and straightened up. 'But I suspect you're glad he's decided not to go through with it, and instead make the place one of their homes.'

'I have to admit I am, although I was worried about how it would affect the locals until Giselle told me he's bought the Parkers' derelict old place and is turning that into a farm park.'

'What a man will do for love,' Nico said lazily, something in his voice setting her senses on high alert. Just in time, she stopped herself from looking up into his face. 'Do you ride?'

Surprised, she told him, 'I'll have you know you're speaking to the five-year-old novice rider of the year at the Parirua Pony Club.'

He contemplated her with a lurking smile. 'I can just see you—that glorious mane of tawny hair subdued into pigtails—'

'Oh, please,' she interrupted brightly, her stomach clenching at the lurking sensuality of his lingering survey, 'even at that age I knew better than that. I had it tucked into a neat little bun.'

'And did you take ballet lessons too?'

'Yes,' she admitted. 'My mother drove us to the nearest town twice a week for ballet and piano lessons. We had every advantage she could possibly give us for kids who lived in the back of beyond.'

He gave her an unexpectedly searching glance, as though he'd registered some hidden pain in her words. He didn't remark on it, however. Instead his gaze travelled past her to the panorama beyond, and he frowned, his eyes narrowing. She began to turn to see what he was looking at, only to freeze at his abrupt command.

'Don't move.' He straightened up and walked around her so that he was between her and whatever he'd seen.

'Why?'

'Because I said so.'

Something in his tone stifled her automatic indignation. Without moving his gaze from the seascape beyond, he reached into his pocket and pulled out a cell phone. He spoke into it in the language she now recognised as Illyrian, his voice low and forceful.

When he'd finished he stood for a long moment still staring out to sea, his ice-grey eyes intent and piercing, before relaxing. 'All right,' he said, and snapped the phone shut and switched his gaze back to Leola.

'Sorry,' he said mildly. 'I noticed something that didn't seem right, but it's just a fisherman who's lost his net overboard.'

She turned to see a brightly coloured fishing boat in the bay below, and the small runabout that had gone out to intercept it.

'Are you expecting trouble?' she asked, immediately concerned for Giselle's safety—and his.

'No,' he said instantly. 'I thought it might be an over-eager paparazzo. Roman is loved and respected here, at first for our father's sake but now for his own, and Giselle is possibly safer here than she was in New Zealand—certainly safer than you are in London.'

Leola should have relaxed, but a barely perceptible note in his voice warned her that he was avoiding the issue. One glance at his uncompromising face told her it would be useless to press him to tell her what was going on.

So she said, 'I don't really wish an incident or bad weather on anyone else in the world, but it would be nice if the press could find something else to concentrate on beside Giselle and Roman's engagement. If I hear the word Cinderella again—or I'm asked once more what sort of dress I'm planning for her—I might do something drastic. Especially since media people have already tried to bribe seamstresses and stylists and anyone else who might have inside access to sell any sketches or photos.'

He grinned. 'Calm down. Nobody's going to die if the design is published before the wedding.'

'On the contrary,' she said grimly, 'someone will die all right. Trust me on that!'

His laugh was marred by a sardonic inflection. 'We're doing our best to make sure that the media is kept at bay. I know how important your career is to you.'

As important as yours is to you, she thought.

'That,' he said, 'is a very interesting expression. Mind telling me what you're thinking?'

Smiling, she lied flippantly, 'I'm thinking up a really good way to kill anyone who might steal the designs.'

She expected him to either probe further, or to make some equally flippant reply. Certainly, the icy sense of withdrawal in his eyes shocked her.

However, his tone was sardonically amused. 'Murder is never a good way of solving problems.'

'I'll bet whoever killed the dictator here thinks it was.'

Leola didn't know what she expected—certainly not a silence that lifted the hairs on the back of her head. It stretched for several seconds too long. For some reason she kept her eyes on the seascape beneath, but her skin tightened and she felt the impact of danger.

CHAPTER NINE

AND then Nico said, 'It's believed he died of a stroke.'

'Did he?' Leola watched him through her lashes. 'I was told he was actually assassinated, and the stroke story was put about by the junta that took over from him.'

'Who told you that?'

Something in his voice made her wary. 'I was researching costume in the national museum in the capital to see if I could get any inspiration for Giselle's wedding gown. One of the librarians mentioned it. She did say it was just a rumour—but she said if it had happened like that, the man who killed him was a hero, whoever he was.'

He said levelly, 'It *is* just a rumour, and I'd be glad if you didn't encourage it by spreading it.'

'OK.' Was she imagining things, or was he really delivering what sounded very like a threat?

He went on with no notable change of tone, 'And did you find any inspiration for Giselle's wedding dress?'

'I hope so. I don't want to claim a heritage she doesn't have, but I'd like to work in some reference to Sea Isles folk costume without being pretentious or condescending.' She changed the subject abruptly. 'Why did you ask me if I could ride?'

He looked a little quizzical, but said, 'I keep several mounts here, and they need exercise. I wondered if you'd like to ride up into the hills with me.'

Leola knew she should say no. In fact, she opened her mouth to do just that, and was surprised when she found herself agreeing. Weak, she thought angrily, weak, weak, *weak*!

Still, in three days she'd be gone, and what could happen in three days?

Fifteen minutes later she was making the acquaintance of a charming bay gelding who enthusiastically ate the piece of fruit provided by the kitchen.

'He's called Happy,' Nico told her, straight-faced, and gave her the Illyrian word for it.

'It seems a very suitable name,' she said gravely.

'Do you need a hand up?'

She shook her head, and vaulted into the saddle. Happy took her arrival on his back with perfect composure, barely moving. 'I assume he's the chosen mount for any novice rider,' she said. Or any woman Nico brought here. 'Why do you keep mounts here? I thought the villa belonged to Roman.'

Nico's horse was a rangy grey, showing some Arabian influence in spite of its size. Once out of the stable yard he said, 'It's mine. Roman asked if he could borrow it because he thought it would be more restful for Giselle than the castle in town.'

'It's certainly beautiful,' she murmured, looking up at the tall, square tower of ancient stone.

'Romanesque,' he said casually. 'It started off as a fortress in the Dark Ages. It's always been the traditional dower house for the widow of the previous Lord of the Sea Isles.'

All those ancestors, Leola thought wryly—named,

numbered, their deeds written up, stretching back beyond the turbulence of the Dark Ages to link with the nomadic peoples who'd settled in this lovely land.

Whereas after years of research a distant cousin had been thrilled to trace the Foster family tree back as far as the eighteenth century to a family of yeoman farmers living placidly in rural England.

But even without those splendid forebears Nico would have been a man to reckon with. She glanced sideways, noting his hands on the reins, relaxed yet controlling; he was an excellent horseman.

Echoing her thoughts, he said, 'The years of training at the pony club paid off. You ride like a Valkyrie.'

'Wildly, singing at the top of my lungs and with an orchestra playing madly in the background?' She laughed, and after a moment so did he.

'No,' he said. 'With complete control of your mount and gracefully, as though you and the horse are part of each other.'

Well, two could play at giving compliments. 'Those ancestors of yours who rode in from the east a couple of millennia ago handed down some of their skills. You're more than good.'

'They turned themselves into sailors very quickly once they reached the Isles,' he said, adding with a wry smile, 'The first Magnati made their living as pirates.'

Leola gazed around at the steadily climbing land. Cicadas sang fiercely in the pine trees, and the scent of the needles lifted the heavy heat that lay over the island. They were high enough now to see more islands stretching south, hundreds of them separated by straits of shining sea until the dim silhouettes merged into the horizon.

Yes, she could see the Magnati as pirates. 'Until they saw the light?'

Nico grinned. 'Until the Prince of Illyria forced the issue after Alexander the Fourth stole his sister,' he said dryly. 'As she was not only pregnant but very much in love with her captor, the prince had to agree to their marriage. He ratified the position of Lord as hereditary, going to the eldest son in each generation, but he insisted the islanders give up piracy and take up shipbuilding and fishing and other more respectable methods of earning a living.'

Leola laughed. 'That must have been difficult,' she teased. 'All that testosterone wasted on fish.'

His sideways glance sent an erotic shiver down her spine.

'I doubt if they wasted any testosterone,' he said, pulling up his horse on a flat area beside an ancient little church. From there they had a magnificent view out over the countryside, green with vines in their stony white enclosures, and beyond to the sea.

Leola fought her treacherous response, all wildfire and darkly dangerous magic. 'You said they were happy together, the princess and her pirate.'

'He never looked at another woman once he'd found his true mate; it's supposed to be a Magnati characteristic.'

But not for him, she thought. Leopards didn't change their spots, and he'd shown no desire to be faithful to one woman.

And because that thought hurt she said brightly, 'So I don't have to worry about Giselle.'

'Trust me, Roman has found his true love. And I'm certain it's the same for your sister.'

'Yes,' she said simply. 'I've never seen her like this before—transformed, almost. I still find it hard to believe that for him she's prepared to endure a very public life so far from home, a situation I'd have thought she'd have avoided like the plague. She has to be absolutely besotted with him.'

'Good.' He leaned towards her to point out the main channel that led to San Marco. 'I was informed that she's led a very secluded life.'

'Hardly secluded—it was busy and full of responsibilities. And who *informed* you?' When he didn't answer she burst out indignantly, 'I suppose you had her vetted.'

Nico's hooded glance conveyed a cool warning. 'I'm very fond of my brother,' he said evenly. 'Naturally I wanted to make sure he'd chosen well.'

'Of all the cheek!' she spluttered. 'And what would you have done if you'd decided she wasn't right for him? Try to buy her off? I'd give a lot to see Giselle's reaction if you did.'

'It would have been interesting,' he agreed with a smile that revealed he'd taken her sister's measure. 'Almost as interesting as my brother's response when he found out. But I'm rather insulted; buying people off is a crude last resort and by now you should know me better than that. I'd only do it as a last resort,' he said thoughtfully, before adding, 'And before you get too carried away, I'll bet as soon as you heard of their engagement you wanted to see them together so you could decide for yourself whether or not Roman was worthy of her?'

Leola, who'd done exactly that, gave him a glittering glare. 'Of course I did, but not so I could put a spoke in their wheel. I just wanted to make sure Roman would make her happy. And you didn't answer my question: what would you have done if you'd decided Giselle was wrong for Roman?'

Enjoying her fiercely protective reaction, he said evenly,

'I'd have tried to break them up.' He ignored her outraged gasp to finish, 'If I'd succeeded, then they wouldn't have been suited; if I failed, I'd have wished them well.'

'Of all the arrogant, cold-blooded, overbearing men, you are the absolute worst.' Her cheeks were flushed and the look she shot him sizzled with scorn. 'How dare you think you had any right to do that?'

'Of course I had the right—he is my brother. I owed it to him to make sure he wasn't doing anything stupid.'

'From my admittedly limited knowledge of him, he's not the sort of man to make snap judgements or injudicious decisions,' she flashed.

Nico grinned. 'Far from it, but men as clever and as experienced as Roman have been known to think with less intellectual parts of their anatomy before.'

When she looked as though she was deciding whether or not to deck him, he relented. 'The moment I saw Giselle I knew they'd both chosen perfectly. Roman isn't going to get away with his Lord of the Isles routine with her, but she'll find that he's every bit as tough and strong-minded as she is.'

Leola shot him a challenging stare. 'Some people find her too astringent.'

'Then some people don't understand her,' he said promptly.

'And you think you do?'

'Enough to know that she loves my brother to the point of adoration. Which,' he finished, 'is probably bad for a man who's already got enough self-assurance without having it reinforced in spades every time his woman looks at him.'

Leola stared at him, saw a lazy grin he didn't make any effort to hide, and said with resignation, 'You've been winding me up.'

'A bit,' he admitted. 'You fire up in your sister's defence so brilliantly. Did you know that when you're angry those amazing eyes have glinting specks of gold in them, like a vein of ore through turquoise?'

Stunned, Leola realised her mouth had dropped open. She closed it with a snap and bit back a caustic retort.

How could he do this to her? Turning her head away from his too-perceptive scrutiny, she pretended to scan the view.

Nico's effect on her had been instant and fundamental—like lightning or an earthquake—rearranging her life and altering her in some way she couldn't explain. The first time she'd seen him she'd been terrified, but she'd responded to his intense magnetism, allowing it to override her instinctive caution.

That awareness had swiftly transmuted into sexual tension, more potent than anything she'd ever felt before.

Bleakly she recalled the aftermath of that crazy night in Paris. She'd been so sure she'd be able to banish him from her mind. Ha! She still dreamed of him, dreams of hope and desire, despair and pain, of a frantic search for something she'd lost and would never find again.

This would be the last time she'd agree to anything so silly as being alone with him. At least after the wedding, except on the odd family occasion, she need never see him.

'Another interesting expression,' he commented. He indicated the plain below and the sea, a vivid skein of blue threading through the multitude of islands. 'When I think of the Sea Isles, I think of this scene.'

'Is that the mainland?' Leola asked, pointing to a dark smudge on the horizon.

'Yes, that's Illyria.'

Leola's brows lifted. 'And this is not?'

He shrugged. 'Old habits die hard,' he said. 'We're loyal subjects of Prince Alex, but we still separate San Marco and the Isles from Illyria.'

'I like that. In New Zealand people who live in the South Island call themselves Mainlanders. They're an independent lot too,' she told him, wondering at the slick of steel, like a blade, in his tone.

Without preamble, he said brusquely, 'The jury is still out in the trial.'

'What? Oh. Of course.' She felt foolish that she'd forgotten. 'The people-smuggler. Do you think he'll be found guilty?'

Nico shrugged. 'He still has a considerable following here in the Isles, which is one of the reasons the trial was held on the mainland. Even without your testimony there was enough evidence to convict him, but juries are chancy things.'

Leola stared at him. 'Was there ever any chance that I might have to give evidence?'

He met her eyes, his own cold and unreadable. A bird chirruped above them in the branches of a cypress, then flew noisily off, its passage marked by a flash of scarlet.

'If it had appeared that the case was going against the Crown, then yes,' he admitted.

'You could have told me,' she said angrily.

'Why? So you could worry about it? I wanted your name and presence kept out of it unless it seemed that the case wasn't strong enough to win on the evidence already presented against him. That didn't happen; the prosecutors had a damned good case.'

Leola opened her mouth to speak, then closed it again with a snap. He might have lent her the protection of his name and his house and his security men, but he had no right to make decisions for her. She flicked the reins and Happy started off with a slight jerk, only to stop immediately when a lean brown hand caught the reins below his head and held him still.

'Get down, please,' Nico said.

Leola's head came up. 'Why?'

'I want to show you something.'

'And I want to go back.'

'Not yet.'

She met ice-grey eyes with defiance. 'That sounded ridiculously like an order.'

Nico didn't let the reins go, but he smiled crookedly. 'I very much want you to see this.'

Mutiny warred with a wish to give him what he wanted; the softer emotion won. 'I hope it's worth it,' she warned, swinging down from the saddle.

He tethered the horses to a convenient tree and said evenly, 'Only you can say.'

This was a cemetery separated from the little church by walls of the same honey-amber stone. Cypresses grew apparently at random amongst the tombstones. It was very still, very warm, with bees browsing sleepily around the flowers that poked out of every available crevice.

'This way,' Nico said.

Her anger dissipating in the peaceful serenity of the place, Leola followed Nico through the old churchyard to an extension where the tombs were almost new.

'My parents,' he said, indicating a grave to one side.

Not knowing what to say, she glanced up at him. He'd withdrawn into some distant place, the angles of his face hard and controlled. The only inscription on the stone gave the names of his parents and the dates of their births and deaths.

Leola looked around. Frowning, she looked more closely at the nearest tombstones. The birth dates were different, but, apart from his parents, all bore the same date of death—around the time the dictator had died.

'What happened?' she asked quietly.

'Roman and I wanted our parents buried in this place, and the relatives of the men here agreed.'

That wasn't what she'd asked, but she waited, keeping her eyes on the tombstones. There must, she thought, be at least fifty or sixty of them. A disaster? A massacre? The hot, sleepy atmosphere seemed incongruous in the light of such wholesale killing.

Still in that cold, flat voice, Nico resumed, 'The dictator died in the castle in San Marco. When they heard about it the locals started to celebrate, and his guards rounded up every man they could catch, lined them up against the castle wall and shot them.'

Her indrawn breath hurt. Without thinking, she reached for his hand. His fingers closed around hers, gripping so tight she almost gasped. He must have felt that tiny involuntary flinch, because he relaxed his grasp, though he still kept her hand in his.

In an oddly dispassionate tone he went on, 'They threw the bodies into the sea, but all were found and brought here, buried together because they died together. When Alex came to the throne we asked if we could move our parents' bodies to this place, and the families consented. It is an honour for my parents.'

'I imagine their families found some comfort in the fact

that you and Roman wanted your parents to lie with them,' she said quietly.

'My father always felt that he should have stayed and fought for them.'

Leola stooped and picked a cyclamen flower, small and white and innocent, from a crevice at the bottom of the surrounding wall. She laid it on the grave.

'I'm sure he's peaceful now.' She hoped it was the right thing to say.

Nico was silent for a long time, his sombre gaze on the small flower already wilting in the hot sun. 'I hope so,' he said at last.

They resumed their ride, travelling further up into the pine-scented hills. The sad story of death had muted that aura of edgy challenge in Nico, and, although they talked of other things, Leola knew that the minutes they'd spent in the churchyard would be etched in her mind for ever.

She now understood the two brothers' drive to help the islanders who'd suffered so much. It seemed their father had somehow transmitted to them his feeling of having betrayed his people by fleeing.

The ride ended at a pavilion high in the hills, overlooking what appeared to be another arm of the sea. 'It's a freshwater lake like the one at Osita,' Nico told her as they watered the horses. 'There are deer in these hills, and Paulo Considine liked hunting in comfort. He had this place specially constructed, and came over to the island to hunt from it, but he was killed in the city before he ever saw it.'

'So it's unpolluted by his presence.'

His smile was grim. 'Yes.'

The terrace in front of the pavilion had once, so Nico

informed her, held the slender columns of an ancient temple. The worn stone pavement contrasted with the sleek modernity of the building behind.

Nico had brought food—a simple snack of fruit and the delicious goat cheese of the island, with a Thermos of hot coffee. They ate outside, sitting on the sun-warmed stones with the fresh, pine-scented air whetting their appetites.

And because the atmosphere was once more fraught with challenge, Leola applied herself to being a tourist, admiring the view, chatting brightly about the islands, about her work, about anything except the one thing that set her nerves tingling—the seething, unbidden attraction that vibrated between them.

Although Nico followed suit, he knew what she was doing. Every so often she saw the glint of mockery in his eyes. The sooner they left here, the better, she thought.

Once she'd drained her coffee she jumped to her feet and walked across to the edge of the terrace, pretending to admire the view.

'Would you like to walk down to the lake?' Nico asked.

When she hesitated his smile hardened. 'You'll be quite safe. There are no pirates around now.'

Only one. She thought a little desperately that anything would be safer than this tense, perilous inactivity. 'Yes, let's go down to the lake.'

The pathway through the trees was narrow, so she stayed closer to Nico, so close that as they were passing a thicket of bushes he was able to catch her arm.

'Wha—?'

He clamped his other hand over her mouth and bent to breathe in her ear, 'Not a word. Follow me as quietly as you can.'

Heart thumping, she did. He slid noiselessly at right angles from the path through the sun-dappled undergrowth with a skill that made her uneasy. Some metres into the brush he stopped and slowly turned, a lean finger indicating a patch of bushes.

Hardly daring to breathe, Leola stared through the leafy tangle of branches, eyes widening as she realised with incredulous delight that she was looking at a doe, golden-brown in the sunlight, suckling her tiny fawn. The doe's head was turned towards them, and she was obviously wary.

'Don't move,' Nico whispered.

Silently they watched the tender, almost too intimate scene until the fawn lifted its narrow head and stepped away, its impossibly long thin legs surprisingly steady.

The doe snatched a mouthful of grass, then picked her way through the trees on the other side of the tiny clearing, mother and fawn disappearing into the darker shade of the pines.

Leola lifted a glowing face to the man beside her. 'That was wonderful,' she said in a hushed voice. 'Why are they so tame?'

'No one's hunted here since Paulo Considine died,' Nico said, his gaze darkening.

When he lifted her chin, she met his intent, half-closed eyes with a fierce demand of her own. Leola knew what he intended, but she didn't move. The hunger that had been building inside her ever since she'd watched him walk back into her life through the castle gardens in Illyria burst into an urgent, pleading need that wouldn't be denied.

CHAPTER TEN

'LEOLA?' Nico's voice was deep and sure and arrogant.

'Yes,' she said without hesitation.

He bent his head and kissed her—not with the ardent passion she craved, but almost tenderly.

Her heart blocked her throat; gently, sweetly, she responded as though they had never kissed before, as though the ecstasy they'd shared had only happened in her dreams.

And then he lifted his head, and disappointment chilled her heart. A noisy clamour of common sense at the back of her mind demanded that she step back, say something bright and inconsequential, put a closure to this thing between them once and for all.

Deliberately, she stayed where she was.

He astounded her by lifting her hand to his lips. The kiss burned her palm, and he held it against his heart afterwards, searching her face with the concentrated attention of a hunter.

Leola stood with bowed head, absorbed in the thudding of his life force—as fast and heavy as her own pulse echoing in her ears. Longing ate into caution, dissolving it like the sun on morning mist.

'How long has it been?' he asked, his Illyrian accent a little more marked, his tone hard with male intent.

'Since what?' Her voice sounded dreamy, almost dazed, and she had to force her eyelids up.

'Since we last kissed?'

She knew to the day, but she said vaguely, 'Months.'

'Too long.'

Too long, her heart echoed wildly. She stiffened at the smell of elemental danger, and shook her head, trying to clear it.

Nico said grimly, 'Look me in the eyes when you deny it.'

His icy gaze locked onto hers and she went under a wave of passionate yearning.

He was too astute, too experienced in the ways of women not to read her surrender in her face. 'Yes,' he said on a raw note, and kissed her the way she wanted to be kissed, his mouth seeking everything she had to give him.

Yielding to his hard strength, she curved against him, taking comfort from his strength, accepting at last that although this shouldn't be happening it had been inevitable from the moment she'd seen him again.

The drift of his fingers across her breast sent rivulets of fire snaking through her, joining and mingling until she was so hot with desire she groaned in supplication.

'Please,' she whispered as he cupped the curve of her breast.

'Please what?'

In answer she pressed into him, welcoming with an exultant leap of her blood his instant response and the soft grunt that emerged from his throat. He grasped her hips and pulled her closer.

'Here?' he asked harshly.

It seemed right to make love here in the forest, away

from the building the dictator had built, away from everything but the innocence of nature.

And then he frowned. 'No, dammit! We can't—I have no protection.'

So he hadn't planned or expected this. In a way that consoled her. 'It's all right,' she said huskily. 'I'm all right.'

His glittering gaze darkened. 'Why?'

Why? Surely he knew?

Eyes diamond-bright, the gold sparks gleaming, she snapped, 'Because I don't seem to have much resistance where you're concerned, and I knew we'd be meeting again. It struck me as a wise precaution.'

He laughed in his throat, the triumphant amusement of a man who was totally confident, and kissed her angry mouth again, wooing it with subtle seduction.

Against her lips he said, 'I'm sorry. I know I have no right, but I was jealous—I thought you might have found someone else.'

Outrage warred with the honeyed sweep of desire. 'Do I look like someone who'd kiss you like that if I was in love with someone else?' she asked fiercely.

'No,' he said. 'You look like someone who's furious, and rightly so. Let me make amends for my crass assumption...'

She glared at him and muttered, 'When I'm with you I can't even think properly.'

He gentled his hold, resting her cheek on a broad shoulder. Sliding her arms around his waist, Leola wondered why she felt so safe. Although, she noted with a secret inner thrill, his body hadn't slackened at all; he was both protective and passionate.

'Proud, possessive lioness,' he murmured into her hair. He

was silent for a moment, before saying with a short laugh, 'We can do one of two things. Either we call a halt right now and steer clear of each other until this damned inconvenient passion withers, or we give in to it for however long it lasts.'

No mention of love, of any sort of shared future.

Shocked by a chill of dismay, Leola hesitated. He was just being honest. He'd always been honest with her.

She made the mistake of looking up, and something twisted in her heart when she met his eyes, almost amused yet flinty. Once again, he was insisting she make the decision. That inner caution warred again with desire; yes, she decided, ignoring the small voice that whispered she was playing with fire. Because she didn't love him, she wasn't risking her heart.

And she wanted him with every fibre of her being.

Quietly she said, 'Why aren't you sweeping me off my feet?' You know you could, her tone implied.

His mouth thinned. 'You can ask that here—with Paulo Considine's hunting pavilion just up the hill? Force achieves nothing worthwhile, and that sort of seduction is a form of force. I don't value what isn't given freely.'

A small, lopsided smile curved her lips. 'Does that apply in your business dealings?'

'If possible,' he said promptly.

'And when it's not?' His faint, intensely personal scent clouded her brain; his warmth and strength surrounded her in mesmerising security.

He said tautly, 'In business I try to make sure that everyone is happy with the results. It's not always possible, so I take the welfare of the greatest number into consideration. Do you want this to be a business deal?'

'No!' Why couldn't she just accept what he was offering without this constant battle between brain and body?

'I'm glad of that, because I don't feel at all businesslike right now.'

Yet still he didn't move.

One part of her was glad he had the will to resist the enormous tide of sensation that surged between them, but another—more foolish, more romantic—part longed for him to yield without thought, to surrender to the tide of passion with no care for the consequences.

He searched her eyes until she thought he almost reached her soul; parrying that intense, metallic gaze took every ounce of self-control she had.

'So—what is it to be?' he asked on a driven note.

'Surrender,' she said in a small smoky voice.

'Whose?'

She managed a soft little laugh. 'Surely it can be mutual?'

'I like the sound of that.' And he kissed her again, lifting her as their lips met and carrying her further into the small clearing where the grass grew soft and thick.

Nico set her down. Flushing, oddly shy, Leola watched him strip off his shirt to reveal lean, sleekly muscled shoulders and the flat plane of his chest and abdomen. Surprised by a surge of passion so violent she couldn't say or think of anything beyond losing herself in it, she forced herself to stand still.

'It's all right,' he soothed. 'I don't think there's anything likely to harm that exquisite skin here.'

She confessed, 'I feel a bit—strange.'

'So do I,' he told her deeply, and eased his hands beneath her shirt, flicking open the buttons as he explored her waist and the soft curve of her breast.

Leola's breath locked in her throat. Obeying her instincts, she leaned forward and bit his shoulder very gently, then delicately licked the skin where her teeth had met it.

When he shuddered she knew it was going to be all right. To be able to shatter that iron-hard control even to that small extent lent her a fierce, primal confidence.

Against the musky heat of his skin she complained, 'Why do I get the impression that you're a very dangerous man?'

Nico froze, then eased up her chin, holding it in a grip that didn't hurt, but that she instinctively knew she wouldn't be able to break. His eyes had frozen, too, into slivers of ice.

His voice was level and toneless. 'I thought I'd shown you that you've nothing to fear.'

'I'm not afraid of you.' She frowned. 'You're dangerous because you can smash my sensible principles into shards.'

He examined her face carefully, and although she could have sworn not a muscle moved in his big body, she sensed him relax. 'It's the same for both of us,' he said, his voice deep and rough. 'I'm sure as hell terrified of you.'

The kiss was a statement of power, of desire and heat and urgency. She matched it with her own sort of power, and somehow he undid her bra and unfastened her jeans, then, still holding her mouth to mouth and body to body, he slid to his knees, bringing her down with him.

Eventually, of course, they had to breathe, but when he broke the kiss she clung to him, her body pliant and demanding in his arms, waiting for the glory of his love-making.

Still locked together, they lay on his shirt. Beneath them the grass was soft and lush; the sun overhead warmed his skin into bronze. He lifted himself on one elbow and peeled off her shirt and bra, using them to cushion her head. Then he surveyed her, gaze heating when she flushed under that fiercely possessive scrutiny.

'When you're in the sun,' he said, 'your skin gleams as though you've been dusted with gold, and your hair glows.'

He bent to kiss the centre of one breast, and she shivered as he pushed her jeans down. His smile was triumphantly tinged with a desire he kept under fierce, uncompromising control.

Heart drumming in her ears, Leola shivered again at the contrast between her skin, pale and faintly gold, and the tanned hand against her, sending its unspoken messages to every part of her body.

Eagerly, urgently, she longed for him with a primitive need that demanded release. But it was such sweet torment to wait as he removed the last garment from her.

'A couple of hundred years ago one of my ancestors found a statue of Aphrodite, the goddess of love, on one of the islands,' he said, easing her last garment down with the denim. 'You remind me of her; she's made of a soft golden marble, and, as well as being breathtakingly beautiful, she's strong and lithe and elegant.' And while colour ran up into her skin, he added with a smile that smouldered, 'Like you.'

His eyes narrowed when she gave a little choke of laughter. His hand came to rest between her legs, covering her, testing her, and her skin tightened as the hunger built beneath those skilful fingers.

'Great minds,' she said, her voice ragged. 'I was thinking that although your ancestors, like mine, would probably have been called barbarians by the Greeks, their sculptors would have died for the chance to use you as a model.' She leaned forward and walked her fingers slowly across his waist. 'Shouldn't you be taking something off too?'

Nico's smile was a carnal invitation. 'Why don't you?'

Undressing him involved laughter—laughter that faded to silence in an exchange of heated looks, then dissolved into intensity when her reckless caresses stoked the fires that had been building in both of them for the past frustrating, empty weeks.

Encouraged by his response to her touch, by his muttered words, and goaded by the urgent pleas of her own body, Leola explored him, sensuously rediscovering the way his sheathed muscles flexed and hardened when she stroked his back and his powerful flanks, or kissed the spot above his thundering heart, resting her cheek there while her hands made forays further down.

Until he said at last through clenched teeth, 'I can't—Leola!' and twisted, rising to come down upon her with speed and precision.

She shivered at the heat of his loins, the sheer male grace of his body and then he pushed home, wrenching a muffled scream from her as her hips rose involuntarily to meet each intensifying thrust. Such fierce passion couldn't last; almost immediately sensation overwhelmed her, carrying her off to rapture.

He joined her there within seconds, and then collapsed, easing down to pull her half over him while his chest heaved.

A sweet, stupefying exhaustion took her by surprise. Eventually she yawned and said in a drugged voice, 'That has to be the best exercise ever.'

'Certainly the most pleasant.' Amusement coloured his voice; she could feel it through her damp skin, a shiver of humour that echoed in some hidden part of her. He said, 'Rest now for a little while. We'll have to start back to the villa soon.'

On a long sigh she yielded, revelling in the slow rise and fall of his chest, the heat of the sun and the sleek magnificence of him. Stiff, sticky, aching pleasantly in every muscle and joint and ready for nothing but sleep, she'd never felt so good in all her life.

They made it in time for lunch, but only just, and any chance of slipping in without being noticed was doomed when Giselle happened along as they came in through a side door.

Her eyes flew from her sister's hot face to Nico's unreadable features, and after an initial hesitation she said, 'I thought I might have to send out a search party for you. Did you have trouble with the horses?'

'None at all,' Nico said cheerfully, turning the full wattage of his smile on her.

Fascinated, Leola watched Giselle almost succumb, but her twin was made of sterner stuff. She rallied and said with a small smile as she continued on her way, 'Then I'll see you at lunch soon.'

At the top of the flight of stairs that led to the bedroom floor Leola said, 'I sense an inquisition in the not too distant future.'

'What will you tell her?'

'Nothing.' She paused, before finishing, 'And that wasn't the right term, either. She won't pry. We used to share everything but...since she met Roman things have changed.'

'Does it hurt?'

'A little bit, but in the right way. She has him now, and they should confide in each other.'

'Of course,' he said on an aloof note.

She left him at the entrance to her room with a brief smile and closed the door behind her with a small decisive click.

In the bathroom off her room she eyed her reflection with shocked dismay. No wonder Giselle had known immediately what they'd been doing! She'd used a comb on her hair, but it still fell around her face in a witch's tangle, her mouth was slightly swollen and red as a berry, and her eyes were slumbrous, hiding secrets.

At least she'd done up her buttons properly, she thought, flushing again at the memory of how easily Nico had slipped the shirt from her.

And no one could see where he'd kissed her breasts, the faint abrasion of his chin leaving an equally faint pinkness on them...

She smiled dreamily at her reflection, then frowned and straightened up. 'Enough of that!' she told herself brusquely.

What she needed was a shower and some clean clothes and a session with her hair-dryer, as well as some cosmetics to tone down that betraying lip line.

All achieved in record time, she walked down the staircase clad in demure silk the same blue-green as her eyes. After the swift skilful application of lipstick her mouth now looked normal, but nothing, she thought, could hide the way her lips turned up, as though she'd been presented with the most wonderful secret in the universe.

While she'd been showering she'd finally accepted that she and Nico were now lovers. How long it would last she didn't know; that it had no future she understood. She would, she thought with a catch to her breath, face grief and some pain when they inevitably broke up. But she'd deal with that when it happened.

That it would happen was inevitable; his string of past relationships had shown her the pattern.

She walked out onto the broad, vine-hung terrace overlooking the sea. Besides, he'd made it obvious that marriage—to her or anyone—wasn't on his agenda at the moment.

Firmly squashing the sad little emptiness beneath her heart, she walked along to where the others sat. They fell silent as she approached and she frowned.

Nico got to his feet, his expression unreadable. 'No stiffness?' he asked.

Her reproachful glance flew to his face. Surely he hadn't been talking to Giselle about—

Anger morphed into confusion at his smile when he added, 'Giselle tells me it's some considerable time since you rode.'

'The stiffness will come tomorrow, if at all,' she told him cheerfully, 'but I have a touch of the sun.' She looked around. 'I thought Roman was eating with us?'

'He's dealing with a possible emergency,' Giselle told her.

'What's happened?'

Nico cut in, 'Paveli was found guilty.'

'But surely—' Leola began, looking from Giselle's concerned face to Nico's stern one.

He said, 'When Paveli was arrested there were protests here. They were soon over, but Roman and his council worked out a way of dealing with any future disturbances. Right now he's making sure everything is in place. And as Paveli was originally from the south—born on what is now one of my estates, in fact—I'll be leaving in half an hour to fly there. Again, it's just a precaution.'

The lover of the morning had vanished. In his place was a man facing something that could turn into a very dangerous situation. Whatever happened he'd win, but Leola wished she could go with him and—

And what?

Nothing. She had no real place in his life. She was simply light relief and relaxation, she thought bleakly.

CHAPTER ELEVEN

STANDING at her bedroom window, Leola stared blindly out over the garden below. What had been waiting for Nico when he reached his estates in the south? The afternoon had dragged on, interrupted once by another telephone call from Roman.

'No signs of protest this time,' Giselle relayed, 'so tonight's reception will go ahead.' She paused then asked carefully, 'Have you heard from Nico?'

'No.' He had taken his leave quite formally, kissing Giselle's hand with an old-world courtesy, and then turning to smile at Leola. But his eyes had been distant, as though he'd left her behind already.

'Don't worry,' he'd said.

But of course she did, and more so when Roman arrived to tell them that Nico had decided to stay in the Southern Isles and miss the reception.

It turned out to be another huge success; fighting back her tension, Leola noted that Giselle looked magnificent, her milk-white skin matching the satin of the dress she'd chosen from Leola's selection, her black hair held in place by a superb diamond clip.

Eventually the islanders would learn to love her. Certainly amongst this representative crowd of Sea Island dignitaries and their partners there seemed to be no animosity at all, no sign of protest.

She found herself hoping desperately that the people in Nico's southern lands felt the same.

Back at the villa Roman called Nico, then turned to the two women watching him with anxious eyes. 'He's fine,' he said with a smile. 'Everything's calm there too. In spite of Prince Alex's programme of conciliation, the Illyrians have no love for those who once worked for the secret police. As soon as that came out, I imagine Paveli lost all sympathy, even from his family.'

Leola nodded, grateful for Giselle who said, 'Thank heavens. How long does Nico plan to stay there?'

'A few days—just to make sure nothing happens, and then he'll be back to take you to London.'

But Nico arrived the evening before he was expected, walking unannounced into Leola's bedroom. She had spent that day being shown some of the magnificently embroidered peasant costumes, and was sketching, her pencil flashing over the pages of her workbook.

Thinking it was Giselle, she said absently, 'Hang on—I need to concentrate on this; I'll be with you in a moment.'

But something in the atmosphere made her turn, her expression lighting up when she saw him. That first incandescent joy faded as she registered an instant shock. Although he didn't look any different, she knew instantly that something had happened.

'What is it?' she demanded, scrambling to her feet.

He didn't answer, but picked up her sketch pad and

examined it, flipping through the pages as her sense of dread expanded. 'Clever,' he said. 'Is this for the wedding dress?'

She braced herself. 'Yes. I hadn't realised that the costumes here were so different from the mainland ones. I'd like to use them as a reference point. Roman's PA introduced me to several local women who've been more than helpful—in fact, they'd be delighted to embroider the dress.'

For once she couldn't care less about her work.

He nodded, then said quietly, 'We have to talk.'

Heart pounding, feeling sick, she bit her lip. 'All right. Is…is there likely to be trouble?'

'Not yet,' he said bluntly. 'After the revelations of the trial Paveli has few sympathisers, and none who dare show their faces openly. The fact that he was revealed to be a rapist and torturer sickened even his most ardent followers.'

'Then what—?'

His hands clenched at his side. 'He got a message through to me.'

Fear froze her to the spot. 'How?'

He made a dismissive gesture. 'It doesn't matter.'

'What did he want?' The words tumbled from her mouth; she stopped and drew a breath, trying to compose her thoughts and ignore the sickening kick of panic in her stomach. 'He must know you can't—won't—try to change the court's decision.'

'He has what he thinks is a trump in his hand. He knows I killed the dictator and he is threatening to reveal everything if I don't get him a pardon. If he makes it public, Alex—who has been working to bring the rule of law to Illyria—will be forced to take action. Possibly there will have to be a trial.'

Whatever Leola had suspected, it wasn't this. Shocked

and stunned, she closed her eyes for a moment, then opened them to focus on his harshly arrogant features. '*You* killed the dictator?'

'Yes,' he said grimly. 'I believed it was the right—the only—thing to do.'

'When? How old were you?'

'Sixteen,' he said curtly. 'Green as grass, and filled with romantic notions of honour and the blood feud, and utterly, completely convinced that he would eventually kill Roman as he'd had my father killed.' His jaw hardened. 'That, I still believe.'

'I know. Magda told me,' she said numbly.

More than anything she wanted to comfort him in whatever way she could, but one glance at his iron-hard features told her he'd retreated to some hidden fortress where she couldn't reach him. So she said quietly, 'Tell me how it happened.'

'My father told us—Roman and me—of a secret passage in the castle that was used as an escape route in times of war. Roman kept up the contacts my father had in San Marco, so I got in touch with one of them.' He paused, before going on bleakly, 'Actually, with his son Cleto—his father had been arrested by the secret police and presumably been killed. We organised it together.'

'You and *Roman*?' She was horrified that Roman could have sent his brother into such danger.

'God, *no*.' He gave a short laugh. 'He damned near killed me when he found out about it. It's the only time I've seen him lose control. No, Cleto and I. He knew that the dictator was coming into San Marco to go hunting from his new pavilion. It was easy enough to get to the castle with him as my guide. And the passage was still usable. I knew that the dictator always stayed in the lord's apartments, so I made my way to the apartment, carrying my father's duelling pistol, and waited for him.'

His voice was level, his eyes steady, but Leola could see how much effort it was taking to tell her.

Her heart contracting, she said unevenly, 'But? There is a but, isn't there?'

It wasn't a question.

A bleak, humourless smile curved his mouth. 'You know me too well. I couldn't do it. I was afraid of him, I utterly despised him, but I couldn't bring myself to pull the trigger and kill him.'

'Of course you couldn't. You're no murderer.'

He didn't seem to hear her. 'He knew who I was—he actually seemed to find the situation amusing. He taunted me with my father's death, and told me Roman would die shortly, though not before he'd been sent a film of me being tortured to death. I lost my head, of course, and like an idiot came within striking range. He'd been waiting for his chance; he snatched up a knife from a table and attacked me.'

'Go on,' Leola said, her voice thin with anguish. She couldn't bear this, she thought, but she had to listen. It was something that had been eating away at him for years.

His shoulders moved in an infinitesimal shrug. 'He was middle-aged, but he was strong—he'd have killed me if I hadn't learned how to fight properly. And if luck hadn't been on my side. I grabbed the knife and managed to turn it, and we fought like animals until somehow—without my intention—the knife went into his heart. He just looked surprised. I was horrified, and I yanked it out...and he died.'

Appalled, unable to comfort him or help, Leola watched him walk across to the window and look out for a few seconds.

Without turning, he went on steadily, 'I got away from the castle and Cleto took me back to Italy. I managed to convince myself that I'd freed the Illyrians from tyranny.'

'You had.'

'Only to wish a worse fate on them,' he said in a frozen, fierce tone. 'You know what happened in the aftermath of his death. But not only the people in San Marco suffered. The military junta took over, and their repression was every bit as bad, with the added misery of civil war as the generals fought each other.'

'At least the Illyrians had more hope than they'd had under the dictator,' Leola said, knowing it was useless.

Ignoring her, he went on, 'Killing him solved nothing; the Illyrians weren't free until they took matters in their own hands and chose their own prince to rule them.'

'And that probably wouldn't have happened at all if the dictator had still been alive,' she said, wondering what she could say that would help him. 'Nico, you weren't to blame for those deaths—the people who committed them are.'

'Nothing can alter the fact that those innocent people would still be alive today if I hadn't killed Paulo Considine.' He lifted his chin, his eyes cold and level. 'I am a murderer, Leola.'

'You were a sixteen-year-old kid brought up on mediaeval traditions of war and honour, a kid who was fighting for his life,' she returned crisply, not giving herself time to think. 'You'd lost your parents tragically, and you were afraid your brother would be the next to die. I'm sure you knew you were probably on his hit list too. Yet when it came to it, you still couldn't kill the man. Would you kill anyone now?'

'If anyone I loved were threatened, quite possibly.' The words cracked out into the room like whips. 'It's no use, Leola. I am what I am, and I can't change the past.

Which has now caught up with me, because Paveli is threatening to reveal everything if I don't get him a pardon.'

'How does he know?'

'Cleto—who ferried me from Italy and back—was picked up by the secret police as soon as he arrived in San Marco again, and disappeared like his father. I assume he was tortured to tell what had happened, then killed.'

Leola had been sure that she couldn't feel any more helpless, but she had to fight back the urge to retch. 'By Paveli?'

'If not him, then certainly on his orders and he made sure the torturers never had the chance to tell anyone else what they'd learned. He may well have seen the information as some sort of insurance policy.'

She whispered, 'What are you going to do?'

After several seconds of silence he looked at her, his expression so utterly remote she almost cried out. 'We spoke about *noblesse oblige* once and you were suitably scathing, but to me it means something. I owe a blood debt to the families of all those who died because of my hot-headed belief that I could save them. When Alex asked us to come back to Illyria, I thought I could expiate that debt by using my money and power on the islanders' behalf, but do you think I'll be able to do anything for them once they know that I was responsible for so many of their men dying?'

'I don't know,' she said unwillingly.

'I do. I refuse to give Paveli the opportunity to regain even a fragment of his lost prestige. I am going to admit what I did, and let what happens, happen. I'm leaving for the capital tomorrow morning to tell Alex.'

Leola saw nothing but bleak, inflexible determination in the slashing contours of his face. Panic was smothered by an aching, inconsolable grief. She drew in a ragged breath, forcing the words out like stones. 'And what do you want me to do?'

'You're going back to London tomorrow with Giselle.' His voice was cool and steady, almost forbidding in its total lack of emotion. 'I'm sorry, Leola. I shouldn't have let our mutual attraction develop beyond a flirtation.'

She flinched. Anguished feelings jostled inside her, preventing her from finding any words.

Still in that sternly uncompromising voice he said, 'There is still danger, so if you stay here you could be a target. I'm sorry I got you involved in this; I thought I could control things, but my actions have made it worse for you.'

Leola had no weapon against his implacable integrity and any protests would only prolong the agony. Although she'd do anything to lighten his burden, it seemed nothing but retreat would satisfy him.

But if she had to lose him, she'd make sure he never forgot her.

'Very well then,' she said quietly. 'I'll go back to London. But I want something from you first.'

His eyes narrowed and he paused. 'Anything I can give you with integrity,' he said.

Head held painfully high, heart hammering so loudly she could hear it in her ears, she met his darkened gaze. 'One last night together.'

His hands clenched at his sides. 'You don't know what you're asking.'

'Are you refusing?'

'I—damn you, no.' He swore in Illyrian, then said in a tight, goaded voice, 'No, it seems I can't refuse you.'

'Sex wins,' she said in a brittle voice she didn't recognise.

'Sex?' His voice was a savage growl. 'Is that all you think it is? Do you really believe I'm tearing you and myself to pieces because of sex? Very well—if that is all it is, let's enjoy it one last time.'

A lethal, silent lunge brought him across the room. Before she had time to do anything but gasp he caught her in his arms, his eyes black with rage and lust and something she thought might be grief.

His kiss wiped every thought, replacing them with a ferocious desire that sprang to life at his touch and consumed her when his mouth took hers.

What followed was violent, urgent and primitive, a fierce melding of mouths while he stripped her. Her hands were just as busy, wrenching open the collar of his shirt, the belt at his waist, passion throbbing through her as they kissed and kissed again, shedding clothes without thought.

Always before she'd felt that he was holding something back; this time—this *last* time—he let go, summoning an equal wildness in her that rose up to meet and match his strength. Her fingernails scored his shoulders; he laughed in his throat and picked her up, one arm clamped across her back, one hard against her hips so he could thrust deeply into her.

She cried out loud, and he thrust again, and this time she convulsed around him, soaring into ecstasy.

When her shudders had died away he asked roughly, 'Are you hurt?'

'No,' she said in a cracked voice. 'You couldn't hurt me.'

He almost threw her on the bed and came down on her again, his mouth avid and eager as he sought her breasts, his hands both soothing and tantalising. 'Don't touch me,' he commanded.

This time he brought her to rapture with his mouth and his skilful fingers. Shuddering in the ecstatic aftermath, she pressed small, lingering kisses along the sleek skin of his shoulder. It filled her with a fierce exultation to feel the muscles flex beneath her lips.

Eventually, taking her time, she reached the tight peak of one of his nipples. It hardened, and she licked it delicately before treating the other to the same, her mouth hot and silken and demanding against him.

'No,' he said through his teeth. 'It's too much...'

'Tough.' She pushed him back, taut and virile and tanned against the white sheets, before beginning to stroke him, studying his face while her fingertips drifted across the hard flow of muscle. Sweat sheened his skin and his ice-grey eyes darkened, turbulent as storm clouds, his jaw tightening as she eased closer to the proud centre of his loins.

Almost angrily he brushed her hand away, then held it tight when she resisted.

'Not unless you want to unman me now,' he said gutturally.

'Not yet,' she told him.

Eyes black in his arrogant, drawn face, he muttered, 'In you. I want to be in you.'

'Good.' Her voice as hoarse as his, she added, 'Because I want to be around you.'

She mounted him, bending to kiss his mouth, his eyes, the sensitive lobe of his ear while she settled herself onto him.

This time his hands clenched into the sheets, his big body taut with the effort it took him to reimpose control.

Inside her, tiny muscles contracted and relaxed, and she began to establish a rhythm, slow and seductive, watching his face as rills of fire ran through her, burning her up. Her breath came faster; she saw his lashes droop, before he forced them up again.

Eyes locked like bitter enemies, they strained together, until finally an exquisite wave of passion swept her over that limitless horizon and into bliss, into ecstasy so bittersweet she felt tears flood her eyes.

Nico thrust deep into her in one final surge, a feral growl erupting from his throat, his hands loosening their grip on the sheets to grasp her hips and pull her down onto him as he joined her in mindless rapture.

Bonelessly she collapsed, so wrung out with sensation and emotions that she couldn't speak. His chest heaved beneath her, his arms clamped her against him as though he'd never let her go, and the sound of his breathing was harsh in her ears. To her appalled shock tears filled her eyes and kept coming.

'Dear heart,' he said in a raw voice. 'Leola, my proud lioness, don't—I beg of you.'

'It's all right,' she wept, furious with herself. 'I'm sorry—this is stupid.'

'I will remember every tear you shed for me,' he said, and kissed her through them, his mouth sweetly seducing, his arms around her.

That was when Leola realised that she loved him—that life without him would be an eternal desert. She'd been too afraid of love to trust herself—or him—and had tried to ignore it, but it had grown inside her anyway and now she would never be free.

Even if Nico were able to ride out the coming storm it would kill her to be just his mistress.

'How is everything?' Leola asked, lifting her eyes to the grey London day outside.

On the secure phone line Giselle's voice sounded oddly disconnected. 'Fine so far. You've seen the papers, I suppose?'

Leola shuddered, her gaze returning to the headlines in the previous night's newspaper. 'I can't avoid them; Roman's housekeeper delivers them to me every morning and evening. Are you all right?'

'Safe as houses,' Giselle said cheerfully. 'Roman was just being a fusspot.'

Roman had tried to insist his fiancée go to London with Leola, but Giselle had flatly refused. Leola was glad the gamble had paid off. Regulating her tone, she asked coolly, 'How is Nico?'

'He's put himself in the hands of the justice system and he's living with Roman under some very loose arrangement a bit like house arrest, but I don't think anyone in Illyria blames him for what happened. In fact, most of them seem to be delighted that he killed Paulo Considine. He's being treated like a hero.'

'He'd hate that.' She was avid for any crumb of information about him.

'I suspect he does, but you wouldn't know it. He's gone into himself—very stern, very controlled.'

Leola's heart contracted in her chest. 'What about the people of San Marco? They were the ones who suffered most after the dictator was killed.'

'Roman seems sure that no one is going to blame Nico for what the secret police did, and from what I've gathered the feeling in Illyria is that he helped bring an end to the bad days.' Her voice faltered. 'Lollie, we have no idea what they went through. The other day an old widow held up her grandchild to him, and shouted, "See, here is my little Tonio. The dictator's men tried hard, but they couldn't kill *all* my family." I felt utterly sick when Roman told me she had only the one son left out of seven.'

Leola asked urgently, 'What did Nico do?'

Her sister sighed. 'He went a bit white around the mouth, but he said something back to her that made everyone laugh through their tears. I'm almost certain it's going to be all right.'

'I'm so glad.'

Leola put the telephone down with a heavy heart. Honour had driven Nico to tell her what he planned to do, and to send her away; she thought he probably respected her, but he'd never mentioned the word 'love'.

Because of course he didn't love her. He was so certain that he was dangerous and unworthy of love that he'd made sure he never got close enough to any woman for it to happen.

'Accept it,' she said aloud.

Wanting was no longer enough—had *never* been enough, she realised. From the first she'd longed for more than transitory passion from him.

So now she loved him—desperately, uselessly, with every part of her.

She couldn't go in to work; the part of the world's press that wasn't in Illyria seemed to be camped outside Roman's apartment in London, intent on making sure they'd be able to photograph her if she set foot outside the place. Originally she'd planned to go back to her new bedsit, but Roman wouldn't hear of it, and now she was glad he'd insisted.

The day she'd flown into London she'd rung Magda to explain, and been told to fax some of her sketches through. It should have been wonderful when Magda rang her back.

'Work them up into designs,' she'd commanded. 'I've got a good, good feeling about this. If you can come up with a few new slants there could be a place for your designs in the next collection.'

A month ago Leola would have been so excited she'd have been dancing, her ambition whipped up into the highest gear.

Now she was pleased, but not thrilled. Surely, she thought in dismay, *surely* loving Nico wasn't going to deprive her of any joy in her creative abilities?

Pushing the phone and newspaper away, she stared down at the final sketch she'd done of Giselle's wedding dress, and without thinking added a slender flounce right down the neckline.

'Yes,' she said decisively. Giselle would complain that she wasn't a frilly woman, but she had a good eye—and eventually she'd see that it set off the whole dreamy, gorgeous dress perfectly.

If she'd stayed in San Marco she could show her sister. But Nico didn't want her there.

Nico didn't want her in any way at all beyond the strictly carnal, and her behaviour that final night had probably convinced him that was the only interest she had in him, too.

Pride, she thought angrily as she got up and paced restlessly across the room, was a cold bedfellow. Once again she toyed with the idea of contacting Nico.

'What part of *thanks but no thanks* don't you understand?' she asked herself out loud, and wondered if he'd used the excuse of his past to send her away nicely, without having to say, 'I don't want you any more.'

Anyway, even if he did want her, any relationship would come to nothing. Designing meant that she needed to be constantly aware of what was going on, keeping an eye on fashion, on fashionable people, on what interested the world she moved in.

She came to a halt in the middle of the luxurious room, seeing nothing ahead but an empty future. 'We could make it work,' she said out loud, and stopped as though she'd spoken treason.

Not marriage—no, not that. He'd want a wife who put him and their children first. But they could be lovers—for a while…

An icy brush against her skin—as though something had happened to Giselle—set her reaching for the telephone, but the feeling faded almost instantly.

Somehow that cold touch of fear made up her mind for her. She loved Nico; he wanted her. And he'd said they'd always been honest with each other. A momentary pang hurt her because of course she wasn't going to tell him she loved him. But she'd contact him, and surely they could come to some arrangement…

When Roman's housekeeper brought in a meal she had to force the food down before glancing at the headlines of the latest newspaper.

Nothing about Illyria this time, thank heavens. With any

luck the whole awful situation would be resolved soon, and she'd be able to get to work.

The telephone rang again. Giselle, she thought with a suddenly racing heart.

No.

Nico—oh, God, *Nico*...White-lipped, she picked up the receiver.

CHAPTER TWELVE

GISELLE's first blurted words were, 'He's all right.'

Leola's blood turned to ice. 'Tell me.'

'It's Nico, but he's OK.'

'What happened?' She could barely get the words out.

'Lollie, he's *all right*! He was attacked, but the knife missed his heart and got his shoulder; he's in hospital having X-rays to make sure it hasn't done too much damage internally, and after that they're going to stitch it, and if I know Nico he'll be out tonight.'

Leola sagged into the chair. 'I—oh, thank God,' she said thinly.

'It was one of Paveli's people.' Giselle's words chased each other. 'He tried to claim it was because Nico had killed the dictator and all his brothers had died—the old blood feud thing Prince Alex has been so determined to stamp out—until the crowd turned on him.'

'The *crowd* turned on him? Where was Nico? Where did it happen?'

Her twin gave a huge, shuddering sigh. 'He was going to church. We all were. It's the name day of the patron saint of San Marco and everyone was there. We were walking up the steps to the church and this guy held out a bunch of flowers. I started to go towards him, but Nico sort of pushed ahead of me, and the man whipped out a knife and stabbed him...' Her voice wobbled.

'You said he was all right,' Leola said, numb with shock.

Her sister gulped back a sob. 'Of course he is. He sort of stumbled, then wrestled the man for the knife w-with blood pouring out of his shoulder. Those damned high-heeled shoes you made me buy!' She gave a half-laugh that sounded suspiciously like a sob. 'I'm not making sense.'

'I don't care, just as long as Nico's all right. *What about the shoes?*'

'I nearly fell over trying to get to the attacker to yank him away, but Roman grabbed me and s-sort of flung me at one of the security men while he and the others ran after the attacker. Nico should have been down, but he—he went after the attacker too. Everybody had been waving and calling out—like the day we first landed in San Marco, remember, when they cheered and threw flowers—but after Nico was stabbed they went quiet. It was so eerie, and then they made another noise—honestly, Lollie, I've never heard anything so blood-curdling in my life.' She gulped. 'I thought Roman was going to kill the attacker, but the crowd got to him first. And as soon as Roman realised he wasn't going to get away, he hauled Nico back and I could get to him to do something about his shoulder.'

In a ghostly little voice she didn't recognise, Leola said, 'It must have been terrifying.'

'I was too busy staunching Nico's wound to see what was going on, but he—the man who attacked him—he was screaming by the time Roman and the police managed to get him away from the crowd.'

'Dear God,' Leola whispered.

'He's in a pretty bad way. Roman said he was yelling—something about Paveli and his children. His own children, not Paveli's. Apparently he kept saying they'd die if he didn't do it. Roman says he's a petty thief but that he's never been in any serious trouble.' She stopped and drew breath. 'I'm not making sense.'

'Enough. Come to London,' Leola commanded, appalled at the naked savagery of what she was hearing.

'No.' Giselle had regained control. 'There's no need. We're all perfectly safe—Nico too—now that everyone knows Paveli for what he is—a trafficker in humans and a murderer. Paveli has well and truly crossed the limits of any loyalty. As far as the islanders are concerned, Nico is a hero. No one will do anything for Paveli ever again.'

Leola bit her lip, desperate to see for herself that Nico was all right. 'He hasn't asked for anyone?'

Giselle hesitated before saying briskly, 'He's been too busy swearing. He seems to think he should have been able to deal with the situation on his own! He and Roman both—what *is* it with these big macho men that they have to blame themselves for everything?'

'Because it's innate in them to protect people,' Leola said, hot tears aching behind her eyes.

Later, when she'd said goodbye to Giselle, she put the receiver of the secure phone down and clutched the edge of the table, breathing deeply while nausea swirled through her in cold waves.

That, of course, was what he'd feared when he'd sent her back to London. And she'd let pride drive her away, because she'd known he didn't love her.

She set her jaw. Nothing mattered now but that she go to him.

How? Credit card, she thought grimly; she'd pay it off somehow. She tried Giselle's number again, but got no answer. Mouth thin and determined, she rang Magda, and when her mentor answered told her what had happened. 'I need to go to him,' she said quietly. 'I'll ring you from Illyria and tell you when I'll be back.'

Magda gave a rich chuckle. 'I've always wanted to be a fairy godmother,' she said. 'Of course. Go to him, and give him my love.'

'Yes, I'll do that.'

He'd probably accept Magda's love. Squaring her shoulders, Leola rang the airline.

In the end it was surprisingly easy to get into the hospital at San Marco—everyone seemed to recognise her. Within seconds she was being greeted by someone who presumably was the hospital superintendent. To her astonishment she was ushered into an elderly lift and escorted to a private room where Nico sat in bed, his features sharpened, his skin paler beneath his tan, a massive bandage around his naked shoulder.

In a chair beside him sat a nurse, who got up as soon as she saw Leola and the superintendent and dropped a quick little curtsey before going out.

'I will leave you now,' her escort said. 'You can stay for ten minutes—no longer.'

Leola swallowed, then realised Nico was watching her, his eyes darkly intent. As the door closed he said, 'How the hell did you get here so quickly?'

She stooped to kiss him, forcing herself to keep it light.

Clearly unimpressed, he lifted his good arm and pulled her close, and she found herself being expertly and thoroughly kissed back.

When it was over, he asked again, 'I asked them to send for you half an hour ago. What did you use—magic carpet? Broomstick? Matter transference?'

Flushed, she pulled back, unable to process the fact that he'd actually asked for her. 'It's taken me five hours! How many stitches have you got there?'

'A few.' He dismissed them with a shrug, but stopped with a wince. 'They're nothing to worry about; the knife managed to miss anything important and as soon as Roman brings me a clean shirt I'll be out of here.' He cupped her chin and fixed her with an intimidating gaze. 'Five hours?'

'When Giselle told me you'd been hurt I maxed out my credit card and got the first flight out.' And although instinct warned her not to, she asked, 'Why did you send for me?'

For long seconds he said nothing, until eventually he said with a crooked smile, 'When I saw the guy spring a knife I thought, *I'm never going to see her again.* And I cursed myself for being a fool because until that moment I'd refused to accept that I love you and need you and want you with me for the rest of our lives.'

Happiness burst inside her like the explosion of some star—fierce and beautiful and so thrilling she could barely contain it. 'I'll forgive you for that,' she said, lifting a hand to his cheek, 'but only because I didn't realise that I love you until you banished me.'

He gave a tight grin, his eyes darkening. 'This is a fine time to tell me, when I can't do anything more than kiss you.'

'Are you sure you're all right?'

'Never better,' he told her, and captured her hand to hold it against his mouth. 'Apart from feeling an utter idiot.'

She frowned. 'It's not your fault! You couldn't know that Paveli would be that desperate.'

'I should have known he'd have another trick up his sleeve after I trumped his supposed get-out-of-gaol-free card by confessing,' he said curtly.

Reining in her anxiety, Leola looked at him. 'What's happening about that?'

He shrugged, then winced slightly. 'Alex got the best legal brains in the country together; they decided that as I'd killed Paulo Considine in self-defence, and as it happened when I was a minor and in a time when all law was suspended, I should be given a pardon. Lexie Considine, Paulo's daughter, went on national television this morning after the ruling was announced to say that she held no animosity towards me.'

'Why?'

Again he sketched a shrug. 'Blood feuds,' he told her succinctly. 'Alex has just about succeeded in stamping them out, but the idea still has an impact on the national psyche. Lexie was brought up in New Zealand and was horrified to find out she was the dictator's daughter, but she went along with the television broadcast so that everything could be neatly tied up. As reparation I'm funding a veterinary college—Lexie's a vet—at the main university in the capital, and a hospital on my own estates.'

So relieved that she could hardly speak, Leola said, 'And that's it?'

'Yes, thanks to the Illyrians' conviction that anyone who killed the dictator had to be a hero.'

Relief soared through her. Although his voice had been wry, he was no longer shutting her out when he spoke of what had happened all those years ago.

She examined his beloved face with her heart in her eyes. 'Everyone does things they despair of in their youth; yours was just more dramatic than most. I bet what the Illyrians admire so much about you is the courage and determination you showed, not the fact that the dictator died.'

'Foolhardiness, more like,' but he smiled at her and she knew that somehow he'd dealt with the horror of the past and was at last able to move on.

He frowned. 'Damn this wound. I can't even give you a decent hug. Do you know that your crazy sister headed towards the would-be assassin, intent on getting that knife off him?'

'Of course she did,' Leola said serenely. 'Although she also wanted to make sure you were all right.'

He sighed theatrically, his eyes gleaming, his smile mock-terrified. 'God knows how Roman and I are going to cope with Amazons as wives.'

Another burst of joy radiated through her. Laughing, refusing to face anything but this wonder, she sat down on the side of the bed and rested her head against his intact shoulder. 'You're big macho men. You'll manage.'

'Do you realise you've just accepted my proposal?'

'I do.' Suddenly serious, she looked up at him. 'Are you sure, Nico? It's not necessary.'

'It is for me,' he said decisively. 'Yes, I'm completely certain. We're going to have to work out some sort of compromise about your career; I don't want you to give up anything for me.'

'It doesn't matter—'

'It does,' he cut in, and lifted her hand to his mouth, holding it there while he said, 'I fell in love with a dress designer and I intend to marry one and have her be the mother of my children. It mightn't be easy, but nothing worthwhile ever is. We'll do it.' His smile was triumphant, a conqueror's smile. 'Hell, right now I could beat the world with one hand tied behind my back! Kiss me so that I know it's real, that you've just agreed to marry me, and that you do love me.'

It was so unlike him to be unsure of anything that she laughed out loud, and was swept into his one good arm and soundly kissed again.

Leola smiled sleepily, groping for her husband who'd just kissed her awake.

'Dear heart,' Nico said huskily, 'the papers have arrived, and I've printed out several online reviews you might be interested in.'

'The baby…'

'Our son is still sound asleep.' The side of the bed sank as he sat down on it. 'Do you want me to read them to you?'

She laughed, reaching up to pull his head down so she could kiss him. After a very satisfactory interlude, she murmured, 'Tell me first whether or not the show was a success.'

'It was a huge success.' His voice softened. 'But you knew it would be.'

Leola said ruefully, 'No, *you* were certain it would be. Magda and I were jittery as hell.'

Yawning, she lifted herself off the pillows. 'And you know what?' she said, smiling at his dark, adored face. 'Although I'm delighted it went well, it's mostly for

Magda's sake. Taking me as a partner was a huge risk for her, but I was determined to keep her reputation intact while appealing to younger buyers. I'm so glad it's worked out.'

She paused, then said quietly, 'There's just one thing…'

His eyes narrowed. 'Tell me.'

'I couldn't be happier, but I sometimes wonder what would have happened if you hadn't been attacked.' Perhaps she shouldn't be asking this; she knew that he loved her, that he was happy. But it had niggled. If it hadn't happened, would he ever have realised how much she meant to him?

One brow shot up as he said dryly, 'I was going to deal with the Paveli situation, then see what we could work out.'

'Deal with the situation? How?'

He shrugged, the scar on his shoulder white and narrow now. 'Take whatever Alex and his council decided, and then come and get you.'

'*Get me*?' she returned, her tone lofty. 'Is that how you thought of it? Behave like one of your ancestors, just grab what you wanted?'

His smile was ironic and tender at the same time. 'Would you have let yourself be grabbed?'

Laughter glinted in her eyes. 'Of course I would.'

His answering smile was slow, pure male intention. 'I suppose the acquisitive, high-handed attributes of my ancestors are still in me. And although I was too slow to understand that what I felt for you was love, trust me when I say that I knew it was different from anything else I'd ever felt.'

She smiled. 'We were both pretty reluctant to accept something that was staring us in the face.'

'Not exactly in touch with our emotions, that was us,' he

agreed complacently, his handsome face far too arrogant. 'The attack sped things up, but I'd have got there.'

Leola's smile turned to laughter. 'Another glorious day in paradise,' she said softly, glancing out of the window.

It was cooler in Osita than it had been in the Venetian-style palace that was their home in San Giusto, and she could see the reflected light from the lake dancing on the ceiling. Her heart swelled. Life couldn't be more wonder-ful. Next door their month-old son lay sleeping in his crib, and her husband was by her side.

'Our little Milan has made a perfect life even more perfect,' she admitted. 'Before I met you designing was ev-erything to me; now it's important, and I'm still determined to make my name, but you and Milan have filled my life.' She smiled mistily up at him. 'Thank you.'

Eyes kindling, he took her outstretched hand and kissed it, holding it against his bare chest. 'You have given me more than I can ever tell you,' he said quietly. 'Love and peace and happiness, and an excitement that will never die—all wrapped up in one person. You make light of the fact that you work so hard for the people of the Sea Isles, using their skills in embroidery in your business, but it would have hurt me if you'd felt it necessary to give it up.'

She drew him down to her. 'You know, I think the papers can wait,' she suggested with a teasing smile.

With a deep laugh he buried his face in her hair and held her close against him.

Before the honeyed tide of passion overtook her again, she said dreamily, 'I love you. I love our baby, I love living here, I love my work, I love everything about life with you, but most of all, I love you.'

Nico went very still. 'And I love you,' he said. 'You give meaning to my life, you make me laugh and constantly surprise me, you deal with my people with such compassion where it's needed and such pragmatism where it's necessary, my heart fills when I see you with our little son, but most miraculous of all, you love me.'

He looked down at her, clear grey eyes no longer icy but filled with intense emotion. Soberly he added, 'And you speak Illyrian with the cutest accent.'

Laughing, they rolled together in a tangle of sheets. This, she thought with incandescent joy as their lips met, was her life, and it was all she'd ever want.

0508 Gen Std HB

MILLS & BOON
Pure reading pleasure

JUNE 2008 HARDBACK TITLES

ROMANCE

Hired: The Sheikh's Secretary Mistress *Lucy Monroe*	978 0 263 20302 8
The Billionaire's Blackmailed Bride *Jacqueline Baird*	978 0 263 20303 5
The Sicilian's Innocent Mistress *Carole Mortimer*	978 0 263 20304 2
The Sheikh's Defiant Bride *Sandra Marton*	978 0 263 20305 9
Italian Boss, Ruthless Revenge *Carol Marinelli*	978 0 263 20306 6
The Mediterranean Prince's Captive Virgin *Robyn Donald*	978 0 263 20307 3
Mistress: Hired for the Billionaire's Pleasure *India Grey*	978 0 263 20308 0
The Italian's Unwilling Wife *Kathryn Ross*	978 0 263 20309 7
Wanted: Royal Wife and Mother *Marion Lennox*	978 0 263 20310 3
The Boss's Unconventional Assistant *Jennie Adams*	978 0 263 20311 0
Inherited: Instant Family *Judy Christenberry*	978 0 263 20312 7
The Prince's Secret Bride *Raye Morgan*	978 0 263 20313 4
Milllionaire Dad, Nanny Needed! *Susan Meier*	978 0 263 20314 1
Falling for Mr Dark & Dangerous *Donna Alward*	978 0 263 20315 8
The Spanish Doctor's Love-Child *Kate Hardy*	978 0 263 20316 5
Her Very Special Boss *Anne Fraser*	978 0 263 20317 2

HISTORICAL

Miss Winthorpe's Elopement *Christine Merrill*	978 0 263 20201 4
The Rake's Unconventional Mistress *Juliet Landon*	978 0 263 20202 1
Rags-to-Riches Bride *Mary Nichols*	978 0 263 20203 8

MEDICAL™

Their Miracle Baby *Caroline Anderson*	978 0 263 19898 0
The Children's Doctor and the Single Mum *Lilian Darcy*	978 0 263 19899 7
Pregnant Nurse, New-Found Family *Lynne Marshall*	978 0 263 19900 0
The GP's Marriage Wish *Judy Campbell*	978 0 263 19901 7

0508 Gen Std LP

Pure reading pleasure

JUNE 2008 LARGE PRINT TITLES

ROMANCE

The Greek Tycoon's Defiant Bride *Lynne Graham*	978 0 263 20050 8
The Italian's Rags-to-Riches Wife *Julia James*	978 0 263 20051 5
Taken by Her Greek Boss *Cathy Williams*	978 0 263 20052 2
Bedded for the Italian's Pleasure *Anne Mather*	978 0 263 20053 9
Cattle Rancher, Secret Son *Margaret Way*	978 0 263 20054 6
Rescued by the Sheikh *Barbara McMahon*	978 0 263 20055 3
Her One and Only Valentine *Trish Wylie*	978 0 263 20056 0
English Lord, Ordinary Lady *Fiona Harper*	978 0 263 20057 7

HISTORICAL

A Compromised Lady *Elizabeth Rolls*	978 0 263 20157 4
Runaway Miss *Mary Nichols*	978 0 263 20158 1
My Lady Innocent *Annie Burrows*	978 0 263 20159 8

MEDICAL™

Christmas Eve Baby *Caroline Anderson*	978 0 263 19956 7
Long-Lost Son: Brand New Family *Lilian Darcy*	978 0 263 19957 4
Their Little Christmas Miracle *Jennifer Taylor*	978 0 263 19958 1
Twins for a Christmas Bride *Josie Metcalfe*	978 0 263 19959 8
The Doctor's Very Special Christmas *Kate Hardy*	978 0 263 19960 4
A Pregnant Nurse's Christmas Wish *Meredith Webber*	978 0 263 19961 1

0608 Gen Std HB

MILLS & BOON®
Pure reading pleasure

JULY 2008 HARDBACK TITLES

ROMANCE

The De Santis Marriage *Michelle Reid*	978 0 263 20318 9
Greek Tycoon, Waitress Wife *Julia James*	978 0 263 20319 6
The Italian Boss's Mistress of Revenge *Trish Morey*	978 0 263 20320 2
One Night with His Virgin Mistress *Sara Craven*	978 0 263 20321 9
Bedded by the Greek Billionaire *Kate Walker*	978 0 263 20322 6
Secretary Mistress, Convenient Wife *Maggie Cox*	978 0 263 20323 3
The Billionaire's Blackmail Bargain *Margaret Mayo*	978 0 263 20324 0
The Italian's Bought Bride *Kate Hewitt*	978 0 263 20325 7
Wedding at Wangaree Valley *Margaret Way*	978 0 263 20326 4
Crazy about her Spanish Boss *Rebecca Winters*	978 0 263 20327 1
The Millionaire's Proposal *Trish Wylie*	978 0 263 20328 8
Abby and the Playboy Prince *Raye Morgan*	978 0 263 20329 5
The Bridegroom's Secret *Melissa James*	978 0 263 20330 1
Texas Ranger Takes a Bride *Patricia Thayer*	978 0 263 20331 8
A Doctor, A Nurse: A Little Miracle *Carol Marinelli*	978 0 263 20332 5
The Playboy Doctor's Marriage Proposal *Fiona Lowe*	978 0 263 20333 2

HISTORICAL

The Shocking Lord Standon *Louise Allen*	978 0 263 20204 5
His Cavalry Lady *Joanna Maitland*	978 0 263 20205 2
An Honourable Rogue *Carol Townend*	978 0 263 20206 9

MEDICAL™

Sheikh Surgeon Claims His Bride *Josie Metcalfe*	978 0 263 19902 4
A Proposal Worth Waiting For *Lilian Darcy*	978 0 263 19903 1
Top-Notch Surgeon, Pregnant Nurse *Amy Andrews*	978 0 263 19904 8
A Mother for His Son *Gill Sanderson*	978 0 263 19905 5

0608 Gen Std LP

Pure reading pleasure

JULY 2008 LARGE PRINT TITLES

ROMANCE

The Martinez Marriage Revenge *Helen Bianchin*	978 0 263 20058 4
The Sheikh's Convenient Virgin *Trish Morey*	978 0 263 20059 1
King of the Desert, Captive Bride *Jane Porter*	978 0 263 20060 7
Spanish Billionaire, Innocent Wife *Kate Walker*	978 0 263 20061 4
A Royal Marriage of Convenience *Marion Lennox*	978 0 263 20062 1
The Italian Tycoon and the Nanny *Rebecca Winters*	978 0 263 20063 8
Promoted: to Wife and Mother *Jessica Hart*	978 0 263 20064 5
Falling for the Rebel Heir *Ally Blake*	978 0 263 20065 2

HISTORICAL

The Dangerous Mr Ryder *Louise Allen*	978 0 263 20160 4
An Improper Aristocrat *Deb Marlowe*	978 0 263 20161 1
The Novice Bride *Carol Townend*	978 0 263 20162 8

MEDICAL™

The Italian's New-Year Marriage Wish *Sarah Morgan*	978 0 263 19962 8
The Doctor's Longed-For Family *Joanna Neil*	978 0 263 19963 5
Their Special-Care Baby *Fiona McArthur*	978 0 263 19964 2
Their Miracle Child *Gill Sanderson*	978 0 263 19965 9
Single Dad, Nurse Bride *Lynne Marshall*	978 0 263 19966 6
A Family for the Children's Doctor *Dianne Drake*	978 0 263 19967 3